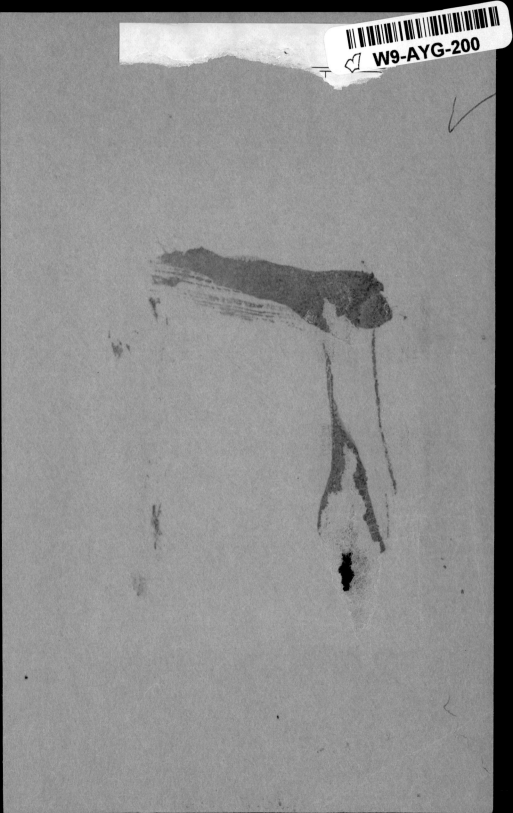

The Leather Hand

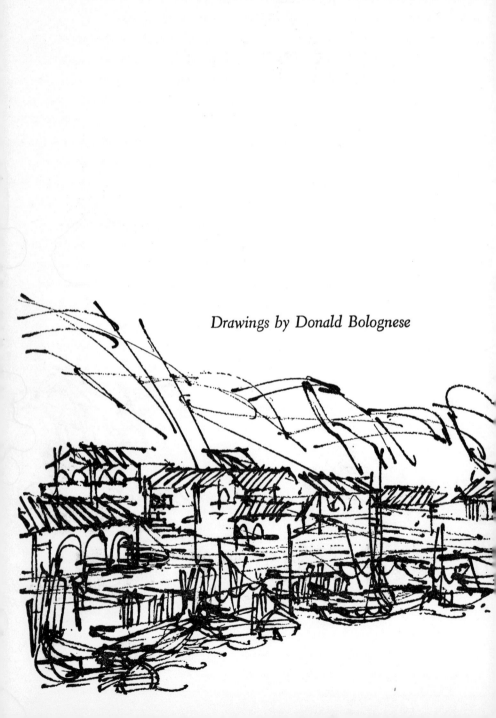

Drawings by Donald Bolognese

The
LEATHER HAND

Anne Sinclair Mehdevi

Alfred · A · Knopf · 1961 · New York

L.C. *Catalog card number 61–6050*

THIS IS A BORZOI BOOK,

PUBLISHED BY ALFRED A. KNOPF, INC.

FIRST EDITION

For my son, Alex Mehdevi

Contents

The Leather Hand

I Go to the Island
of Manacor

   My mother and I called him Jap. The local peo-
ple of Manacor, the Mediterranean island where we
lived, called him *El Japonés*. Perhaps he really was from
Japan; there's no telling, for he never spoke about himself. My guess is that he was Malayan or Filipino. Whatever he was, I liked him. He was a squat, muscular little
man with a face as clean and smooth as a piece of oilcloth, and a silent, withdrawn manner.

He taught me all I know about the sea, about underwater fishing—or skin diving as it's called today. This was
thirty years ago, before undersea equipment could be
bought in every sporting-goods shop. Jap made his own

equipment, and it didn't look like much. He never used flippers or oxygen tanks; in fact, he didn't use much of anything but that incredibly agile, steel-strong body of his and a pair of goggles with a curved tube of bamboo attached for a breather. They were ordinary motoring goggles, I suspect, which he had backed with sponge rubber so they would hold tight to his temples and keep the water out. The breather was the crudest contraption imaginable, about the shape and size of a big candy cane, only hollow. The short end, which Jap shaped by dipping the bamboo in boiling water, he held in his mouth; and the other end (attached to the goggles by a rubber band) stuck above the sea surface like a periscope. I couldn't understand at first how he managed to dive with it, for there was no stopper or trap door to prevent the water from flowing into the tube and into his mouth once he went under. Jap explained: "Human mouth best trap door ever invented. Jap just stick tongue into tube like a cork, then no water gets in mouth." I didn't have to ask how he got the water out of the tube, for after watching him once I knew: every time he rose to the surface a small spray spurted out the top of the breather. The expelling of his breath forced the water up and out.

His single-pronged spearhead was his own design, too. The flanged prong was long and thin; that was its secret —needle-slender but strong enough to pierce without buckling. Jap attached these spearheads to bamboo shafts, weighted with lead so they would carry true as a die under water. He always roughed up the grip with pine rosin so it wouldn't slip.

Jap used to go out daily in a cockleshell of a boat. And in plain sight of the port, the quay, and the main street, he would let himself overboard and disappear with a flip of his feet, coming up in a moment with a fish glistening at the end of his spear. Within three or four hours he had loaded his boat to the gunwales with fish, while in the same length of time the cane and net fishermen caught one tenth as many.

Jap's skill didn't endear him to the people of the port —most of them fishing families. They considered his manner of fishing not quite fair. It eliminated the element of luck which all fishermen believe in and want to believe in. People left him to himself, though they bought his fish gladly enough for his were bigger and fatter—since he could take his choice underwater and select the big ones.

He didn't seem to mind his isolation. He lived alone on his proceeds in a modest stone and mud house, neatly whitewashed, at the edge of town. He had never married, but he had a big dog, Lobo, to whom he was attached. He had taught the dog to eat fish.

How Jap came to take a shine to me I don't know. The local youngsters were set against him; they had heard their parents talk against him, I suppose. But I was a stranger as he was. I was American, and I made no secret of my admiration for Jap.

I used to hang around the dock at two in the afternoon, the hour when he usually came in with his boat heaped with its slippery, shining catch of fish. In his awkward way he sometimes spoke to me in pidgin. This attention flattered me; I asked him endless questions until one day he indicated, with a grin and a flip of his head, that I could come out with him if I wished.

That first day I sat in the boat holding my breath while Jap seemed to stay under forever. I peered into the green, blurry water, trying to locate the white, ghostly shine of his body—scared to death that he'd just stay down there and forget to come up. But soon I lost my fear and was eager to try diving myself. Jap made a pair of goggles for me, and one day in August I—a boy who could scarcely swim except for the side stroke I had learned at the Newton, Kansas YMCA—I saw for the first time the wonder-world of the sea bottom. Jap wouldn't let me attempt a dive the first day—not until he'd taught me about breathing and how to swim with confidence. I just floated on the surface that day with my goggled face in the water and Jap's breather in my mouth.

That first sight of the world beneath the surface of the sea was one I shall never forget, though I'm forty-five now and have seen a good many sights since. Suddenly I was looking down upon a secret topography, the mysterious landscape of the sea—green clad-mountains, purple moors gently heaving with sea heather, sandy valleys, and rocky deserts. And all of them gently swaying and misting before my eyes as if they were being seen through a glass smeared with tinted oil. It gave me a strange feeling, that first peep into the hidden heart of the sea, a feeling that I still get every time I put on the goggles and look beneath the flat, skin-like surface of the water.

The feeling is hard to describe. I felt suddenly alone,

weightless, anonymous. And there was the silence, the world I saw before me was steeped in eternal silence, voiceless—and graceful. There isn't a graceless living thing within the sea world. All movement is languid, sinuous, rhythmical. Even Jap, who walked with a rolling kind of heave on land, his legs bowed, his arms dangling —even Jap beneath the water became a creature of infinite grace, his movements all of a piece, his long hair floating free, his body snaky and prowling.

I've never stayed longer than I could hold my breath, but they say it's a dangerous thing to do, and I understand why. Not that the sea threatens—on the contrary, it lures. It's like an opiate—that taste for descending into the silent, gently rocking underworld. They say you never want to come up once you've dwelt on the floor of the sea; you wander in a dream and never want to stop wandering.

Sometime, lost in the fascination of the sea world, I used to doubt myself, question who I was. Not five months before I had been a member of the sophomore class at Newton High School in Newton, Kansas; corduroy pants, sweat shirt and sneakers. I had never even heard of the Los Campos Islands, where my mother and I now lived. As for the Mediterranean, I certainly never thought I'd explore the bottom of one square mile of it so well that I would know every dent and crevice as well as I knew Arrowhead Junction near Newton.

I was an average boy at high school, not even given to daydreams and travel romancing. I was vain and incurious, wrapped up in myself and my world of drugstore dates, the Uptown Theater, football games and class elections. I had a car—that is, my father let me have the car almost any time I wanted it—and I was seldom home. When I was home, I was sprawled out beside the radio, reading pulp Westerns. (There weren't any comics in those days, nor television either.)

Then one day, one normal run-of-the-mill day like all the others, I answered the ringing of the telephone and heard a voice which changed my life forever. "Is this the home of R. R. Vallings?" the voice asked.

I answered that it was. My father's name was R. R. Vallings. Mine is R. S. Vallings. My first name is Ronald.

"Are you Mr. Vallings's son?"

"Yes."

The voice, a man's voice, hesitated and softened. "Young man, I'm . . . I'm calling from the General Hospital emergency ward. I'm afraid I have bad news. You'd better call a taxi and get down here."

Something inside me faltered; my heart seemed to skip a beat. "What . . . what's happened?"

"It's your father . . . he's hurt . . . fatally, I'm afraid. I'm sorry, son."

The voice stopped. I heard the click of the receiver being hung up. But I continued to stand there holding the phone in my limp hand. I couldn't believe it. I felt a strange impulse to call the man back, to tell him he'd made a mistake. But instead I told the operator to give me the taxi stand and, without telling my mother, rode down to the hospital as if in a dream. I didn't cry until they took me to the stretcher where my father lay with his face covered.

Father had been killed in a freak accident, one of those things one reads about in the papers but can never imagine happening to oneself.

My father was walking to his office on a Saturday in February when a gasoline truck collided with a passenger car at the main crossing in Newton and turned over on him, crushing him instantly. I was the one who had to tell my mother. I was the only child, and we had been a close family. Mother was stunned, inarticulate. Something inside her fought like a tiger against believing the truth. She couldn't accept it.

After we buried father, my mother left his study intact —his scuff slippers under the bed, his smoking jacket on the hook behind the door. Even his desk she wouldn't touch, with its sharpened pencils in the brown pottery jug and the lawbooks stacked to one side. (He had been studying at night to pass the Kansas state bar examination.)

I remember the drifting days and nights that followed, the silences, the long, endless, empty hours. I continued to go to school and mother tried to carry on her housework. But neither of us could shake off an eerie feeling of unreality, of marking time. With father's death the vital pulse went out of our household. We closed ranks, mother and I, but it was no good.

Something had gone out of mother, too. She lost thirty pounds and began to cough. I remember the icy despair that clutched my heart when our old doctor told me that she might contract tuberculosis unless she could stop brooding and put on some weight. I felt her slipping gently, quietly away from life, away from me.

"Nothing to worry about, yet," said the doctor, "but . . ." and he shook his head. "Tuberculosis is a mysterious thing. It takes over if you give it half a chance." He paused and put his finger tips together. "Ronald, you're old enough to be told that we doctors know very little about some things—even now after two thousand years and more of recorded medical history—especially when we have to contend with those mysterious things, the human spirit and the human heart. Your mother is a particularly sensitive person, and it's my opinion that sorrow has made her ill. The TB bug, you know, is in the air almost everywhere; it strikes usually when a person's self-defenses are down. And unfortunately it grows and multiplies unless the infected person's spirit will fight against it.

"I've known your mother for many years, and I've observed that her health is a simple barometer of her spirits. She reacts more quickly than anyone else I know to emotional shock. You yourself must have noticed how her eyes glow and how pearly her skin is when things are going well. And you also must have seen how flushed her cheeks are, how vague and nervous she becomes when troubles wrack her." He paused again. "The usual treatment for borderline tuberculosis is complete rest and idleness, but in your mother's case I'd prescribe the exact opposite—activity, an occupation, as long as it isn't physically tiring. I don't like her apathy, Ronald, I don't like it at all. She's got to get a grip on things. . . ."

After he'd gone I knelt at mother's side. She was in the rocking chair on the sun porch, where she liked to sew and look at the garden through the screens. "Mother," I said, rigid with dread, "Mother, you've got to take hold. Mother, you're abandoning me. I won't let you."

"Oh now, Ronnie, don't get so worked up. I'm all right. Just leave me in peace. I want to rest."

"No. I won't let you rest," I cried, grabbing her hand as if I could pull her back to life by force. "You've got to get up . . . move . . . open your eyes. Mother, mother, I'll . . ." Sobs were choking me. "I'll force you to get well. I'm going to take you on a trip. We're going to climb mountains and explore caves and take an airplane ride. Oh, mother, don't disappear before my eyes. I can't bear it." And I buried my head in her lap.

She stroked my hair for a while. At last she said: "You're right, Ron. I'm being selfish . . . but, dear, I can't pretend. I feel no interest somehow, except in you. And you're big enough now to take care of yourself. You have better judgment than I about most things. I sometimes wonder why I bother to get out of bed in the morning."

Her last words chilled me. I tried to laugh. "Who'll make me wash behind my ears and stop biting my fingernails if you don't get up?" I said. Tears sprang to my eyes.

At this she looked very sad and reached out for my hand as if to comfort me—her hand so dry and hot. "Poor

Ronnie, you're so very young. No wonder you're upset with me. If you could only spare me a little of your vitality. . . ."

"Mother," I said, "I shall, I shall. But you must obey me. You mustn't turn away. Mother, I'll force you. . . ."

"Yes?" she said, then wearily: "All right. Lead me and I'll try to follow, dear. But don't go too fast."

"Oh you're wrong, mother. We're going to run, run away, fly. . . ."

I talked long with the doctor, a family friend who had known mother for years. He agreed that she should be taken away somewhere—far away from father's closet, still filled with his clothes which she neatly brushed once a week; far away from the double bed with its empty half. She must be taken somewhere where she would have to think, to move, to pay attention.

Then one day the doctor came up with an idea. It seemed farfetched at first, but the more I thought about it the more I liked it. A former patient of his, a Mrs. Archer of Wichita, had spent two years on the island of Manacor with her husband, who was retired and liked to travel. Though this couple was well enough off to live there without additional income, Mrs. Archer being a busy soul had looked around for something to do and had hit on the idea of opening a notions shop. It had done surprisingly well. In that primitive society ten-cent store gadgets from the United States appeared to be treasures. There was a continuous demand for them.

"Why not open a similar shop in those parts? Mrs. Archer's experience is almost a guarantee that you can make a go of it—inexpensive odds and ends from over here. I could send you replenishments from time to time." The doctor paused. "As a matter of fact, I helped Mrs. Archer and she never complained about the purchases I sent. I've been here in Newton so long—all the wholesale people know me, and it's no trouble for me, just a phone call. I'd do anything possible for your mother, Ronald, you know that. Trust me to keep you in stock; just send me a post card. And no delays in delivery." He smiled. "I operated on the leader of the local transport union—cancer of the throat—fifteen years ago. He's still going strong and he'll get things to you on schedule, I'm sure."

The doctor went on to describe the island of Manacor. It was in the Mediterranean—a warm, even climate for mother—the second largest of the Los Campos group. The weather was pure and clear and the mode of life so different and strange that mother would feel herself set down in a pioneer's world. Things might make her angry and indignant there, but "that would be all to the good," said the doctor. "Once you get a person mad you can be sure he's taken an interest in what's going on and isn't going to die on you."

When I mentioned the idea of the shop to mother she smiled. Whatever I decided would be all right, she said without a flicker of interest. Determined to force her interest, I began to talk of the things we would buy to stock the shop—celluloid dolls and Philippine beadwork, Indian arrowheads, buttons, needles, pins. . . .

"Isn't that just like a boy?" she said suddenly and

pertly. "That's perfectly silly—pins and needles. They all come from England. Why carry them back across the ocean again? But now, leather things strike me as cheap and good, and tools; they're cheap and very up-to-date, and serviceable. . . ." She paused, pursing her lips.

I was grinning. "Mother, are you disobeying?"

"Well, it's downright silly if you're going to do something not to do it with some sense. I must say, a woman's hand is certainly needed. Pins and needles, indeed!"

I laughed and hugged her. "Mother, let's quarrel," I shouted. "Let's quarrel!" It was the first time since father's death that she had spoken up about anything.

"For heaven's sake, leave go. You're squashing me."

"Come on. Get on your bib and tucker," I said. "We're going shopping for stock."

My heart was singing. For the first time I was full of hope, real hope, that our venture would turn out all right.

Our medicine was good, the doctor's and mine. Mother was, after all, an alert young woman—about thirty-eight, I think, though she would never tell me her age. "I'm past twenty-one, that's all you need to know," she would snap. During the sea voyage she was still listless, but once we set foot on Manacor she rolled up her sleeves, so to speak, and took charge. As our doctor had predicted, mother disliked Manacor at first sight. And it was this dislike which cured her, not the pure, fresh air and the tranquil pace of life.

"It gets my dander up," she would say. "These shiftless people! Why, they don't even know the world is spinning around and has left them behind." Everything about the place irritated her tidy, Midwestern heart. "If you don't keep moving from morning till night—watch out. You'll grow to be like these folks. How they can just sit and stare all day is beyond me!"

The crumbling port, half-silted; the mossy quay, sun-steeped; the gray, grassless hills behind and the liquid-eyed people, always sad, always dreaming—all this struck her as unseemly.

"They'll never get anywhere, I can tell you that," she would say. "I must have been out of my right mind to let you bring me way over here." She meant it, too. But she also was aware of the wakening life in her and didn't suggest leaving. "As long as we're here, Ron," she said, "we might as well make a go of it, show them how Americans do things."

The town we chose to live in was called Puerto Del Sol, which means Port of Sunshine. It was the third largest town on Manacor with a population that I estimated at around two thousand. Mother didn't want to live in the island capital, where the shop might have done better. "These people all look like cutthroats and rogues to me," she said. "The fewer of them around the better. A little town seems safer."

We rented a one-story house and turned the front room into a shop. "Kansas City" mother called it, and we had a sign made and hung it in front the first thing: "KANSAS CITY, novelties; prop., Mrs. R. R. Vallings." Mother scrubbed and whitewashed and made curtains. Our arrival created a stir in town, and our goods—the tools and the yard goods especially—were eagerly touched and coveted. Most people in town had to save for weeks to buy our tools, but they did it, for ours were better than the old ones they had. As for the yard goods, mother had been right to bring them over. Every woman in town was begging her husband for a cut as soon as the materials were draped in our show window. In the first two months we supplied trousseaus for two local brides.

In spite of the fact that the local people took to mother's rosy, open countenance and frank manner, she steadfastly refused to study the language, a Spanish dialect. "What use have I for such a barbarous tongue?" she said. "My goods will sell themselves without any sweet talk, and I can add up figures in any language." However I quickly picked up enough words to handle customers who wanted explanations or information. And all this time, day after busy day, I watched, as if observing a miracle, the glow returning to mother's eyes and the hot, feverish glitter fading away.

We had contacted a local doctor, of course, Dr. Sanchez, who continued mother's treatment. I was able to explain everything about her case to him for he spoke English, having studied in London. I told him mother's reactions to emotional stress were especially strong. In fact, I spoke almost the same words our doctor in Newton had spoken to me. Dr. Sanchez understood, for he, too, was a humble and sensitive person, if a bit old-fashioned. Activity, he agreed, was beneficial to her as long as it was productive and didn't tire her too much. He thought the shop a fine idea for, he said, it was a "creation" and as such a counterbalance to the negation and depression which had made her ill.

Within two months we were firmly established, and mother was growing stronger every day. I had already written to our old doctor in Newton to ship over more tools and yard goods.

I also let it be known around town that we would buy curiosities and handwork from local people who brought them in. This was mother's idea and it was a good one, though in the end it led to all our troubles. She had noticed that excursionists from the island capital, a city of about a hundred thousand people, used to come out to Puerto Del Sol on Saturday or Sunday afternoons to picnic and swim. They invariably stopped to look over the new shop everyone was talking about, our Kansas City. That kind of shopper wasn't interested in ginghams and farm tools but was hungry for the things of the souvenir variety—peasant handcraft, curios, basketwork. So we began to stock the local product—hand embroideries, home-loomed wools, sheepskin rugs, and especially archeological trinkets. These things—old coins, amulets, old tiles—were always being turned up by the farmers' plows or were caught in the dragnets of the fishermen.

The prospect looked good for the Kansas City. Mother and I felt pretty proud of ourselves. "Yes sir, we've showed them how things can be done when you've a mind to do it," she said.

Now that I think back, I see that Señor Valdez helped us more than we realized at the time. He too was a recent arrival in Puerto Del Sol; he also had come for his health.

What's more, he was curiously well-informed about the archeology of the place and intensely interested in all the old Roman and Carthaginian coins that people brought in. It was he who evaluated them for us and told us what price to pay and what to charge. In fact, it was he who gave mother the idea of sending out a call for old coins in the first place.

Being a South American—from Medellín in Columbia—he knew Spanish and found his way around the place quickly. He spoke excellent English as well, which endeared him to mother. "He's about the only civilized being in town, excepting ourselves, of course," she said.

I'll never forget my first sight of Valdez, that first day when he came into the shop two weeks before we had opened for business. He smiled and exclaimed, "Kansas City! You must be Americans. And you'll need help. I'm at your service."

He was a giant of a man with a heavy, furrowed face and a leonine mop of grizzled hair. He looked as if he could tackle a bull—but he was in a wheel chair. It wrenched my heart to see him, that big-bodied man with fierce eyes, a helpless invalid. He had been partially paralyzed by a bullet in some skirmish with revolutionaries in his own country, he said. He never talked about the incident, avoided it, in fact. His left arm was amputated about five inches below the elbow, and he always had a blanket or mat over his paralyzed legs, as if to hide them.

For all his disabilities he was a domineering man, and he moved about well enough in that chair of his. He had brought it with him. It was equipped with a gasoline motor, a steering handle, and gearshift—even a reverse. He could move down the streets at a good clip, weaving in and out among the burros and mules. The town was all on a level, being on the sea, and the houses and shops were all one-story, so there wasn't any place in town that Señor Valdez couldn't go in his "scooter," as he called it. But he couldn't leave the town precincts, for Puerto Del Sol was ringed around by rocky hills threaded by steep and angular paths. The only level path wide enough for Señor Valdez's wheel chair was to a lonely uninhabited spot called Frenchmen's Woods. Still he never seemed to object to his confinement and seemed to find plenty to keep him busy within the town itself.

The chair was fitted with pockets and compartments, as shipshape as you please: places for books, newspapers, snacks, and tobacco; places for an extra pillow or a throw rug in case he felt like napping. A folding writing desk, pens, sunglasses, brandy bottle, and heaven knows what else were in those bulging leather saddlebags that hung under the arms and on either side of his chair back. It seemed to me that there wasn't anything he couldn't carry along with him wherever he went.

Mother took to Valdez at once He was a bit of a gallant with her and he was about her age, maybe five years older. As I say, he helped us get over the thousand and one irritations that were bound to occur when a couple of Kansas strangers tried to get things done in a hurry in Puerto Del Sol. It was he who got hold of a carpenter for us and explained to the man what mother wanted in the way of display cases and counters and shelves. He bullied the electricians into wiring the place so the goods would show up nicely. He informed us where to buy our groceries and what was a fair price.

"I just don't know what I'd do without Mr. Valdez, Ron," my mother would say almost every day.

It was Valdez who sent Paco to us. Though I disliked Paco from the beginning, mother hired him as a handyman and servant. He was about the most miserable specimen of a man I'd ever seen—shifty-eyed, loose-mouthed, and as dumb as an ox. I don't think he ever washed; he smelled of sweat and, frankly, I didn't trust him. I told mother this.

"I don't trust any of these natives," she said. "But I'd trust Paco more'n the others. He looks too blame stupid to think up any connivery. Besides, he speaks English." Actually, I think mother was sorry for him. He was an orphan and, as it turned out, terrified of everything.

Paco's touted Englished vocabulary contained about twenty words he'd picked up somewhere from a cockney sailor. He always called mother "Mum," which tickled her. I spoke Spanish to him myself; my Spanish was better than his English. By threatening to fire him every day if he didn't look sharp, I managed to make him earn his keep. "Aye, aye, sir," he would say, blinking sadly with his big, red-rimmed eyes. He did the heavy lifting, scrubbed the floors, and carried wood and coal for us. He slept on a cot in a small room off the patio.

·　·　·

Before I go into the tragic events which were even then looming over us, I have to say that I never shared my mother's opinion about Manacor. If there were any place like it today, I would retire there and never ask to see the benefits of civilization again. But Puerto Del Sol has kept up with the times, I'm told by tourists who go there in herds now. The airplane and the movies have changed it all.

Thirty years ago it was a drowsy corner left over from earlier times. The women wore faded blue skirts down to their ankles and three-cornered shawls over their braided hair. The men were gruff and manly, drab as dung in their dress, but full of a stern and awkward dignity. They were all dirt farmers and fishermen. Aloof they were, for all their harsh existence—aloof with the pride of men who pit themselves against nature and need make no apology for the bread they've earned.

As for those rock-faced hills that made my mother shiver just to look at them—"They look so naked, like a landscape on the moon," she would say—as for those majestic, austere hills which pushed our fragile, tumble-down port to the edge of the sea, I grew to love them. None of your lush Ohio-valley green for me. I like to feel myself in touch with the earth's bare crust. And in spring there were yellow gorse and purple heather heaped over those rocks, and the odor of rosemary and juniper every-where. The rock hills were harsh, but when they gave of their bloom they gave in full measure, and the contrast made a boy take notice, take account of nature—a thing I had never done back home.

Then there was the sea, the ever-present, ever-audible sea. Being brought up in Newton, I had never seen more water than flows in Turkey Creek. But there will be more of the sea in my story, more of the sea and more of Jap, who taught me to respect and love it.

The Map of the Mary F.

♥ *In recording the events of those days on Mana-*
cor I have been trying to remember their exact sequence.
As I think back, I am certain that my mother and I had
no inkling of the fantastic forces that were converging
upon us until the day Jap brought in the ship model. It
was toward the end of June, almost a year to the day since
we had arrived. The Kansas City hadn't made us rich, but
it kept us alive, and mother's spirits were so even and
cheerful that I never thought about going back home.

I was enjoying myself, though I sometimes worried
about my education. Mother had insisted that I bring
my schoolbooks along, but I wasn't much good at self-

education. I didn't have the application to get down to work. I wanted to be a lawyer, which meant a good many more years of study. And I still had two years of high school to get through. But for the time being mother's health was more important than my career; and like any youngster I felt I had years to spare, years to waste. Besides, I was a year younger than most of my classmates at Newton High, having skipped a grade in grammar school. I kept myself busy and didn't think of the future.

We didn't have the money to go back to the United States anyway. Father had left little besides his insurance. Our house back in Newton had been sold, and all our reserve money had gone into the Kansas City. It had cost more to get the shop in running order than we'd planned on, but it brought in enough to keep us going comfortably and pleasantly from day to day, and we didn't ask for more.

It was June, as I have said, a quiet time in Puerto Del Sol, when the first curious event occurred. Mother and I were alone in the shop on a hot and sultry afternoon; I was arranging a display of shells, visitors from the capital liked to buy them, and mother was knitting. The door opened and Jap came in carrying a package.

"Well, Mr. Jap, I see you have something for me," said mother.

Jap nodded "yes." He understood English well though he spoke it abominably. Jap often brought us *amphorae* and shells which he found on the sea bottom. Amphorae (the singular is amphora) was a word I soon learned; it

was the Latin name for a particular kind of stone or earthern jug used by the ancient Greeks and Romans for holding oil, wine, honey or water. Because Manacor had been on the ancient trade routes, there were many of these amphorae in our waters, lost or thrown overboard over two thousand years ago.

After looking around as if to make sure we were alone Jap unwrapped his package. It was a ship model, a queer, dainty, brittle thing about two feet long. It didn't look like any ship or boat I'd ever seen, and as I found out later it was a model of a Japanese sampan. It was beautifully made, with a palmito shelter or cabin toward the stern, a small scull at the back, and a sail that was ribbed with bamboo lengths no bigger than my little finger. The sail hung on a sturdy mast.

"It's mighty pretty, Mr. Jap," mother said, "but I wonder if I'll find a customer for it. Kind of out-of-the-way looking."

"No sell," said Jap. "No sell. Keep, please. Pretty, see?" And he furled the little sail so that it folded up like a fan.

"You mean you want to give it as a present? You know we never accept presents. You can't do that and keep friends if you're in business."

"No present. Mine, boat mine. But you keep. Look, pretty," he said, moving the scull back and forth.

"He wants us to keep it for him, mother. It's a nice decoration for the shop," I said.

"All right. We can put it up there near the shells where the afternoon sun strikes." She turned to Jap. "All right.

We'll keep it for you, though heaven knows why you can't keep it yourself. I must say, it will be a trial to dust."

Satisfied, Jap nodded and grinned. Then he delved into the pocket of his corduroy pants and brought out a closed fist. Stepping closer, almost crouching, he thrust his hand under mother's nose and opened it. In his palm lay three golden coins.

As mother gave a little gasp, I stepped closer to peer at the coins. I saw at once that these were not the same kind the farmers and fishermen brought in. The usual ones that turned up were Greek or Roman, mostly the latter, and were either brass or copper; they were irregular in shape, having been hammered rather than cast. Jap's coins were perfectly round, with beveled edges, and bore the imprint of an elephant and a castle. They were unmistakably gold.

Jap's black eyes were snapping. He spoke hurriedly: "You smart people. You tell me what is. Read, please. Tell me what money this is."

"Well, we ought to ask Mr. Valdez, don't you think? He knows . . ." mother started to say, but Jap interrupted.

"No. Only you. Ron and Jap friends. No tell others, please. Big secret."

Mother picked up one of the coins and turned it over. I bent over her, trying to read some inscription or date. The coins were strangely clean and new-looking. We were so absorbed that we didn't hear the opening of the door as Señor Valdez entered. He maneuvered his wheel chair towards us. Jap instantly stiffened and put the two

coins he was holding into his pocket. His face was despairing as mother absent-mindedly continued to hold the third coin in full sight.

"Good afternoon, milady of Kansas," said Valdez, his eyes fastening on the coin at once. "I see you're knitting your pretty brows over another farthing that must have dropped out of some Roman legionnaire's money pouch."

She couldn't very well hide the coin, so she turned to Jap. "There's no need to be so all-fired mysterious, Mr. Jap. Mr. Valdez is the one who can help you." She turned back to Valdez. "Take a look at it. Doesn't look so amateurish as those Roman pennies, does it? What do you make of it?"

Valdez took the coin and rubbed it between thumb and forefinger. (He was extremely agile with his single hand, could even thread a needle with it.) He studied the coin intently. I could see he was very excited.

"Where did you get this?" he asked Jap.

Jap looked frightened and sulky. He shrugged. "Don't know. Dog dig."

"Where did the dog dig? Were there any other coins around?"

Jap shook his head.

"Where did the dog dig?" said Valdez, growing impatient in spite of himself.

Jap shrugged again. "You want? I sell. How much worth?"

"No, my good man," said Valdez with a touch of annoyance.

"But I would like to know where you found it. Perhaps

there are more, and you may become a rich man."

Jap sidled towards the door. "No understand. I go now." And before any of us could say anything to stop him, he had slipped out of the shop.

"That chap has found more than he's telling," said Valdez. Though he spoke lightly, his big, lined face was flushed. I could see he was angry with Jap.

"Why?" said mother. "What's there to hide?"

"My dear lady," said Valdez, smiling now, "this is a British guinea, of a kind minted largely in the eighteenth century—to be exact, from 1633 until 1813. It's none of your Roman blobs of brass."

Mother was impressed. "It's a good-sized bit of gold, I must say. You don't see gold coins nowadays, besides its being of antique value. What do you think it's worth, Mr. Valdez?"

"Oh, not much," said Valdez. "Five or six dollars maybe . . ." He paused. "But it's interesting, very interesting."

Mother seemed slightly disappointed. "Well, it's a lucky find for Mr. Jap, I guess, though not exactly a treasure, nothing to write home about."

Suddenly Valdez said: "Are you busy? Would I be interrupting if I told you a story?"

"Why, certainly not," said my mother, folding her hands in her lap. "Is it about this coin?"

"Yes, very much so," said Valdez, settling back in his chair after lighting up one of his special cheroots—very thin and black—which were sent to him from Colombia. "First, you may have wondered what I'm doing in this heathenish place. For my health, yes . . . and no. Weather and sun can't help a cripple like me except perhaps to lift my spirits, which need I add are usually trampled down again by the stubborn idiocy of the people of this . . . this blessed isle. I'll tell you. I came here with a purpose; I came on a hunch, because I'd heard a story that seemed to be worth following up.

"Now, two years ago in Colombia, before my . . . accident, shall we call it . . ." He indicated his amputated left hand. "Two years ago I met an English Johnny out in the jungles near the headwaters of the O——. He was working for the Standard Oil people managing a road gang. He was one of those rolling stones who are so charming when young and so pathetic when they get wrinkles and ailments. Jack Armstrong was his name. He was 'county people,' as the English say, salt of the earth, neither poor nor rich. A bit of a rum pot, Jack was. One night in his cups he told me his story. I want you to picture this if you can: the jungle night; the old rummy, his eyes bloodshot, his voice hoarse; the kerosene lantern between us. Outside, the rustle of the jungle; inside, the guttering of the little chip fire . . ."

I listened with hushed breath as Valdez's words flowed on. They unfolded a story which rang true as silver yet seemed so fantastic, so unbelievable—as if taken from some saga of ancient times. I listened enthralled.

The story Valdez told was this: Jack Armstrong, who was sixty when Valdez knew him, said there was a legend in his family, a legend which promised wealth and power to the person who could understand "the map of the

Mary F." This was a piece of paper on which were traced in faded ink the outlines of a bay, surrounded by hills.

"I have the map," said Valdez. "I'll show it to you in a minute. Armstrong sold it to me for a case of French brandy. Unwise of him, I believe, for I think it was the brandy that killed him; he died soon after."

My mother was visibly shocked. "How can you talk like that, so cold-like, Mr. Valdez?" she said. "The poor lonely man. You should have put him in the hands of a competent doctor instead of selling him hard spirits."

Valdez half bowed from his chair. "Milady, *are* there any competent doctors? And anyway Armstrong had reached the end of the line. These drunks are intent on slow suicide and won't be foiled. But to go on. The map of the *Mary F.*, I found after I got my hands on it, was only half a map. It had been torn in two and the left-hand half was all Armstrong had. Beneath was written: 'Fat Jack, his half.'

"Jack Armstrong's great-great-grandfather was Fat Jack. He was a sailor, a boatswain on many a ship, as it happened, during the mid years of the eighteenth century he was boatswain on the *Mary F.*, a two hundred-ton frigate of the Royal Navy that carried supplies and mail from England to the British garrison at Port Mahon on the island of Minorca. The British were in possession of Minorca from 1716 until 1756, when the French laid siege from both land and sea and captured the port. Now in June 1756, the very day of the surrender of the British forces—June 28th it was—the *Mary F.*, unaware of the danger, was tacking into Port Mahon with a load of supplies including two strongboxes containing ten thousand guineas for the use of the garrison.

"As the *Mary F.* hove in sight of Port Mahon, her officers saw a pall of smoke hanging over the fortress. Georgetown, the British garrison town, was in flames. The mouth of the harbor was completely blocked by a fleet of French men-of-war. The captain of the *Mary F.*, not wishing to risk the gold he carried in a one-sided skirmish with the heavily-armed French ships, decided to withdraw to the nearby Spanish island of Manacor, about thirty miles west of Minorca.

"He put into the harbor of Puerto Del Sol but didn't approach within a mile of the little town. He sent two boatloads of men ashore at a place which has been called Frenchmen's Woods ever since, for reasons which will be obvious in a moment. They were ordered to find water and fill the kegs. No sooner were the English lads ashore than they were ambushed by a contingent of French, who outnumbered them five to one and took them all captive. The French were well supplied with guns and ammunition—evidently a shore battery that had been set up to prevent disabled British ships from seeking refuge in Puerto Del Sol harbor. The French quickly manned a number of heavy longboats and prepared to come out and board the *Mary F.*, forcing a hand-to-hand battle.

"The captain of the *Mary F.* got ready to stand his ground, though, since his was a supply ship, his men were not trained fighters and were badly armed. About a quarter of the best hands had already been captured by the French.

"Meanwhile he ordered the boatswain—that is, Fat Jack—and an ordinary able-bodied seaman named Neddie to take the ten thousand guineas and sink them somewhere offshore in shallow water where they could not be seen from the surface. The two sailors were told to make some record of the spot, so the money could be recovered later. Fat Jack and Neddie did as they were ordered, returning to the *Mary F.* only after the ship had managed to beat off the French maurauders with a terrible loss of life on both sides. There was no doctor on board, and the captain, being a humane man, decided to go back to Minorca to get help for the wounded. He tried to make a run through the blockade around Port Mahon under cover of darkness.

"Well, he failed. The *Mary F.* was sunk. She was only an old supply ship and never had a chance anyway. All the wounded were lost—the captain too. But Fat Jack and Neddie both managed to get away in a small boat.

"There were four others with them including the second officer, who was in command. But Fat Jack and Neddie, for reasons which can be easily understood, decided—silently, I expect, by means of nods and glances—to keep their secret to themselves unless they were asked about it. When the boat finally made it to Fornells, a small British outpost on the north shore of Minorca, everyone was taken ashore. Eventually, after the surrender of the island, the survivors from the *Mary F.* were shipped back home to Portsmouth. Fat Jack and Neddie kept mum.

"They didn't trust each other, though, so they made a map and split it, each taking half.

"As for the official records of that gold shipment, they stated: 'Lost at sea, went down aboard the frigate *H. M. S. Mary F.* off Port Mahon.' After all, no one except the captain, who had gone down with his ship, and the two sailors, Fat Jack and Neddie, knew that the gold had been removed from the *Mary F.* before she sank.

"Unfortunately Fat Jack fell on hard times and was never able to go back to Manacor. When he was an old man he used to tell his story over and over again. Many people thought he was a bit daffy. But when he died the map was found among his effects. His grandson—in other words, the grandfather of the Jack Armstrong that I knew —believed the story, as boys will believe any tale of high adventure. After he grew up he made strenuous efforts to track down the other half of the map. He found that Neddie *had* gone back to Manacor twenty years after that fateful day but had been unable to find the gold. Neddie's heirs knew nothing about the gold or the map. They thought the whole tale a sailor's cock-and-bull yarn. Neddie himself had died of a fever at Puerto Del Sol.

"Now in old Fat Jack's effects there were several letters. No one had bothered to look at them until the grandson began his search. He found that they were undated, though the postmarks were legible. All had been dispatched during the summer of 1776. They were signed with an X, but they must have been from Neddie. Their contents seemed to prove it. Evidently Neddie was illiterate and the letters had been written for him by someone else. They were vague, because Neddie probably didn't want the writer to know what he was talking about. All of the letters made more or less the same appeal: 'Jack, send me your half. I swear I'll bring your due back to England. I can't get my bearings without your half. For God's sake, be a trump, Jack my lad.'

"But Fat Jack evidently didn't trust Neddie; it appears that he never sent the map or a copy of it. The last letter from Neddie ran: 'Jack, the fever has got me. But I'll get the ups on it, never fear. I'm expecting your half by the mail boat every week, Jacko. But if it's in the cards that I pass in my checks, I don't want the Papists here to get their hands on the bright-and-shiny. I hid my half in Frenchie's Woods at the very spot where they got poor Spudsy. God bless you, lad.' "

Valdez paused in his account. My mother exclaimed softly: "Poor Neddie." As for me, I held my breath, waiting.

"Well," said Valdez, "the long and short of it is that no one ever found Neddie's half of the map. I've been digging around in Frenchman's Woods for almost a year, and I've found—exactly nothing. That fool of a Neddie probably stuck the map under a stone or something, unprotected, and it's disintegrated in the century and a half that have passed since then. Frankly I had hoped through perseverance to find the gold without the second half of the *Mary F.* map."

He paused and tapped the coin excitedly against the arm of his chair. "Now this guinea, this is a find." He leaned forward, his voice growing softer. He was almost whispering. "This can't be anything but Fat Jack's gold. It *can't* be anything else." He stressed each word, speaking slowly, tapping the coin again and again. "It can mean only one thing, don't you see? Our secretive Japanese has stumbled on something. Either the hoard itself or Neddie's map."

In the silence that followed my mother said, "Mercy!"

"It means wealth, riches for the man who finds the mates to this coin," said Valdez. "I've checked the records. Fat Jack's story rings true. There *was* a ship, the *Mary F.* And she *was* carrying a consignment of gold— ten thousand guineas. Ten thousand of these golden baubles, enough to buy this town lock, stock, and barrel. And they're somewhere here near us, lying untouched underneath the very waters you swim in every day, Ronald!" A flush had risen in Valdez's seamed cheeks. He touched my arm lightly and went on, his voice gentle and persuasive: "Now you, Ron—the Jap likes you. You could help me. Talk to him; get the secret out of him. Find out where this coin came from. Find out. You can do it, Ronald. The Jap doesn't trust anyone but you. You won't go unrewarded, I promise you."

My heart was pounding with excitement. I was sure Jap would tell me his secret, sure I could wriggle it out of him. Valdez saw he had won me. He held out his right hand to clasp mine. "It's agreed then," he said. "I've told you all I know—and I've never told anyone else. There isn't another living soul who knows about this map. We'll be partners, Ronald."

I was reaching out to shake his hand and seal the agreement when mother spoke rather sharply. "Just a minute, son. Don't you think that gold belongs to Mr. Jap if he's found it? What about him?"

Valdez's hand remained in air. I dropped mine awkwardly. Valdez's fierce eyes seemed to pierce me for a moment; then he shifted in his chair, withdrew his hand, and turned smiling to mother.

"Milady," he said rather too graciously, "don't trouble yourself about the little man. He undoubtedly can't find the gold without me. He may have run across one or two stray coins, but he needs my half of the map to find the bulk of it." He paused. "Of course, if he could be persuaded to cooperate, the gold would be fairly divided." Valdez didn't sound convincing.

"That seems fair," said mother, taking him up. "Why can't Ron ask him to join forces with you and . . . ?"

"Ah yes, of course," said Valdez. "But . . . you will not tell him what I have told you, naturally." The glint in his eyes made the chills run up my spine.

"No, I won't tell him," I said.

"Of course Ron wouldn't go babbling," said my mother tartly. "He's an honorable boy. But I'd just as soon he doesn't get mixed up in this. He's Mr. Jap's friend and he's yours and I'd like him to stay that way. We don't need any money anyway," added mother. "It's

been my experience that too much money is only a nuisance."

Valdez smiled. "I agree, madam. And so Ronald will
remain my friend and Mr. Jap's, as you call him. . . ."

"I'm sure he can persuade Mr. Jap to join forces. It
would be silly not to, since neither of you can find the
gold without the other, it seems—if there *is* any gold.
Sounds mighty unlikely to me."

Seeing that mother's objections had been answered,
Valdez reached into one of the side compartments of the
chair and withdrew a leather wallet. "Perhaps you'd like
to see Fat Jack's map?" he asked, looking directly at me.

Mother clucked her tongue. "Well, I always say what
you don't know don't hurt you." But Valdez had already
unfolded the yellowed paper.

As he spread it out on his knees, I bent eagerly forward
and my eyes fell for the first time upon the map of the
Mary F. I was trembling with excitement, peering intently at the faded blue ink, which Valdez traced with his
forefinger as it formed the unmistakable line of the western shore of Puerto Del Sol bay. Many years have gone
by since that day, and I've wished many a time that I had
never set eyes upon that brittle old piece of paper. It had
already cost the life of one man—poor Neddie; and it was
to cost the life of another, a far greater man. But a boy
has no head to think of such things, and I looked at the
paper with a quick-beating heart.

It was the crudest of maps, sketched out evidently by
Fat Jack himself in some secret session with Neddie over

ATALIA

FRENC
Woo

NORA'S
BEACH

N

Off Shr Fr Wd

Shtst Gr
Atalia
at 90°
to

PUERTO
DEL
SOL

Fat Jack: his ½

a tallow candle. I have made a copy of it here as I remember it, for later the map was lost.

As anyone can see, there was little to go on without the missing half—only the bearing ninety degrees, but, since the second point of the bearing was missing, that left one the whole of the bay to make angles from. The Atalia was a Moorish watchtower, still standing and easily identified. Frenchmen's Woods was also easy to find, though it was too diffuse to be a bearing point. There was no indication where the gold might be, no cross nor arrow. An incomprehensible legend, torn away at the right edge, read:

Off shr Fr Wd
shtst gr
Atalia
at 90°
to

3

Neddie's Half

Mother kept the guinea. Jap didn't come to collect it, and when I asked him if he wanted us to sell it for him his face clouded over, his eyes shifted away, and he said nothing. I confess I brought up the subject often enough, curious as I was and half suspecting that Valdez was right about Jap's having stumbled onto Fat Jack's and Neddie's pile. I even thought I might wheedle Jap into being friendly with Valdez—bring them together in partnership, I thought, with a nice commission for myself. Like the young fool I was, I had the idea that gold hunting was like some commercial deal. And I thought Jap a bit pigheaded, the way he closed up tight. His

40

smooth, waxy face would purse up and his eyes grow
blank every time I dropped a word about the guinea.
"Forget money, Ron," was all he would say.

As for Valdez, he didn't bring up the map again to me.
I took it for granted that he thought me a sort of namby-
pamby, too much tied to my mother's apron strings to be
of any help as a confidant. However, I had given him my
word that I wouldn't reveal his story to anyone. And having bound me he bided his time.

"It's just as well they aren't pestering you about that
map, the two of them," my mother said. "You'd be
caught in the middle, Ron, if there really was a heap of
gold."

I continued to see a lot of Jap. It was summer and we
went fishing almost every sunny day. I had become almost as expert as Jap in diving and throwing the spear. I
could go down ten yards and hold my breath a good minute and a half, corking the breather with my tongue.
Some people dive without breathers nowadays, I'm told,
but they're only handicapping themselves. With the
breather you don't have to lift your face above water when
you come up, and so you can keep the fish always in sight.
Many a time at the beginning I lost a five-pound fish by
lifting my face out of the water to breathe. Mediterranean fish are wily and experienced; I've seen red mullets
change to green in a few seconds when they're hovering
in a clump of green seaweed.

The spear was a tricky thing, but once I got the wrist
technique it was easy. Such spears are called Hawaiian
slings today, though the Japanese invented them. There

was nothing to the spear—an eight-foot length of bamboo, a metal head, and at the blunt end a loop of rubber. (Jap used half an old bicycle inner tube, split lengthwise.) You slipped your hand inside the rubber loop and then nudged it up along the spear shaft until the rubber was taut and the shaft half out behind you. To shoot, you merely let go—more manageable and more accurate than the air-pressure guns they use today.

We used to shove off in Jap's little boat shortly before dawn. Lobo, the dog, always tagged along to the dock with us but Jap never took him out. "Dog is guard dog," he explained. "Guard his master. Nothing to guard against at sea." When we returned, though, Lobo was still there on the dock, sitting on his haunches exactly as we had left him hours before. Jap used to give him a raw fish as we touched the quay, and Lobo gobbled it up, bones, head, and all.

Though Jap and I never spoke much, a strong sense of friendship grew up between us just as it often will between two men devoted to the same task and doing it together side by side. It is odd, now that I think back on it, our closeness. He, illiterate, as unpretentious as a child; and I, somewhat bookish and prone to flights of ambition. We even looked as different from each other as two human beings can: I, a great, lanky, thin boy, blond as a wheat shock, and Jap, small, knotted, his skin burned dark by years of the sun. There were twenty years separating us, but our mutual love for the sea spanned them easily.

Sometimes we spent whole mornings together without

exchanging fifty words. We needed no words, for we felt a fraternal bond that was beyond expression. We two were the only ones who knew the secrets of this sea floor; the knowledge made us brothers. The sun shone down upon us equally as we sat together in his little cockle boat; the sky cupped us close, within the immense circle of the bay. We were freed of all pretenses—two human beings who needed only to smile or grunt to understand each other. I knew I could trust Jap with anything, and I felt in return a deep fidelity toward him.

I was half glad, to tell the truth, that the British gold seemed to be forgotten. Even to mention it to Jap made me feel somewhat deceitful; I could not reveal Valdez's story, and keeping it from Jap made me feel disloyal to him somehow.

But unfortunately gold can never be left to lie forgotten. One morning Jap showed up at the dock with a severe bruise on his cheek. His left eye was swollen and the skin of his cheek bone split open. He said nothing until we had rowed out of earshot of the quay. We were alone on the sea, far out, when he shipped the oars and looked at me.

"Jap scared," he said. "Someone try rob Jap last night."

The idea struck me as ridiculous and if it hadn't been for his puffy face I would have laughed. There was no one in Puerto Del Sol who lived more modestly than Jap. He possessed no valuables at all except the two gold guineas, which would hardly be worth the risk of jail for a thief.

In his staccato way he told me what had happened. Though his language was clumsy, his understanding was acute; somehow he was able to convey all he wanted to say. He had gone to bed at sundown as he always did, locking his dog, Lobo, in the woodshed. He never locked his house doors, though as a rule he shut them and left them on the latch. But the air had been sultry and hot that evening and he left the patio door ajar—it opened onto a field—to create a breeze. About midnight he awakened suddenly with a feeling of apprehension. He didn't know what woke him; the house was silent. He lay still, listening, tense, when a shadow blocked the faint light from the patio doorway and a man entered. "Great big man, giant man." The man walked soundlessly to Jap's closet and began to go through his clothes and belongings. Recovering from his surprise, Jap shouted and leaped out of bed. The man whirled and struck him across the face, one blow, which felled him. Lobo, the dog, began to bark wildly in the woodshed, scratching and yelping to get out as the intruder hastily slipped away through the patio door. "I see his back. Head touch top of door. Biggest man I ever see," said Jap.

"But why should anyone try to rob you?" I said. "Did he take the two guineas?"

Jap shook his head. "I no got them. I throw them in sea, out deep. Money mean trouble."

"You threw them away?" I said, unable to hide my surprise. Jap worked fifty or more hours underwater to earn the value of a single guinea. Why had he simply thrown them away? "What could the man have been looking for?"

Jap looked at me sorrowfully for some time. Then he patted his heart. "Jap got secret, heavy secret. Weighs like lead." The little man bowed his head as if the secret were an actual weight that dragged him down. I felt sorry for him—the accidental keeper of some secret he didn't want but couldn't get rid of. All the verve had gone out of him; he seemed bewildered, lost.

He lifted his head and went on. "I want give secret away. I want give secret to you, Ron. You my friend. You take?"

"Gladly, Jap," I said, and when I said this I was truly thinking as a friend would think, only of relieving his misery.

"You young, Ron. You want be rich like all young peoples. You don't know yet, don't know every piece gold on earth cost many lives."

It was then that I realized what he was about to do— give me the key to the British gold. He was going to *give* me the gold. He didn't want it himself and would perhaps have preferred to let it lie undiscovered. But someone else was after it, and now that he couldn't just go on and leave it where it was. The gold must be uncovered, or his pursuer would never let him rest.

"It's no good present I give, Ron," he said, shaking his head. "But you young, you like, yes?"

My excitement showed on my face. I confessed it. I was a hot-headed youngster and the thought of treasure was like wine. It made me dizzy. The wide world seemed to open up before me—travel, cars, a fine home for my mother. But it wasn't really what the gold would buy that made my heart leap; it was the excitement of it, the joy in adventure.

Jap said: "You home tonight?"

"Yes."

"I come see you. Eight. You alone."

I told him I would see him in my room where we would be alone.

All at once, then, he seemed to forget about it. He busied himself with putting on his goggles and preparing to dive. The salt water stung his cheek wound badly, so he stayed in the water only a short while. Our catch was small, just enough to split between us for supper.

As we rowed home my mind was whirling with a hundred thoughts. Jap spoke only once: "I going find big man which hit me. Wear gloves, that big fellow. Hit me with glove. Glove very heavy, like lead pipe. Jap find him. Jap eye very quick, see much."

I tried to imagine who it could have been. Of course I thought of Valdez, who was a big man who was deeply interested in the treasure. But his being paralyzed ruled him out.

Suddenly I thought of the gin-shop man. They called him Gordo. He was a husky fellow, two hundred and fifty pounds at least, and an evil-looking person to boot. He was big-mouthed and lawless; he fancied himself a kind of freebooter because he'd been a smuggler in his younger days. He had broken plenty of laws in his time, I suspect, but he was a great one for talking about honor. "I never put a drop of water in my booze," he would say, "and I never will. I'm an honorable man. My wine isn't full of chemicals and dyes like the swill the other crooks sell." His bully-boy honor had been offended by Jap, and Gordo made no secret of his antagonism. Whenever Jap passed the gin shop, Gordo used to wring his meaty hands together and say: "I'll wring his neck someday, the little yellow mannikin, the little sneak." Gordo's father was a fisherman whose income had been seriously diminished by Jap's advent in town. "It's sneaky, the way he fishes, going down and picking them off like berries off a berry bush. I'll skin him, I will."

I had always taken Gordo's mutterings for the usual bluff of the bully. But my mind fastened on him now as I sought a culprit. There wasn't anyone else in town who had spoken so openly against Jap.

I said: "Do you suppose it was Gordo?"

Jap shrugged.

"But what is there to steal?" I said, speculating rather than asking a question.

Jap said one word: "Tonight." Then as if speaking to himself he said: "Gordo, Gordo's papa, Paco—who knows? Could be anyone. Smell of gold to men like smell of catnip to cat. Go crazy, do funny things. Everyone in town know about that guinea I bring you mama."

We usually locked the shop at seven, but I kept the door unlocked until well after eight, waiting for Jap. Finally at eight-thirty, when he hadn't showed up, I locked up and went to my room, more disappointed than I wanted to admit to myself.

There he sat on my bed, pleased as punch with himself. "How did you get in?" I said.

He grinned. "No one see," he said. "Jap silent like a swimming fish." Then his moonface turned serious. "You got sampan, yes? Bring, please."

I went into the shop and brought back the model sampan he had left with us. He took it and deftly dismantled the sail, lifting the mast out of its socket in the hull. The mast was hollow, a tube of bamboo. From inside he withdrew a tightly rolled piece of paper—yellow, brittle, terribly old.

Before he drew it out, even before my eyes lighted on that paper, I knew in my heart what it would be—Neddie's half of the map of the *Mary F.* And I knew that I should not look at it. The other half, Fat Jack's, which I had seen a scarce thirty days before, was still clearly recorded in my mind. And if I looked at Neddie's half, I would be the only living person to have seen both, the only living person able to find the gold.

But the temptation was too great. I crouched over the little man, my eyes staring at the piece of paper he was so slowly unrolling. Jap began explaining in his laconic way how he had stumbled on the map; my impatience mounted. It was hard for Jap to convey a series of facts with the few words at his command; his voice, toneless, seemed to struggle on and on, groping for meaning. I forced myself to listen while all the time my eyes, my heart were fastened upon his square hands that were carefully unrolling the paper.

"Funny thing. Accident. Jap out fishing for deep-water

fish near north shore," he went on. I listened. He had been fishing when his spearhead jammed against a rock under the water. When he pulled it loose the prong was bent. He clambered ashore at Frenchmen's Woods to straighten it out. And there, there at the water line under a rock he found the map and the three guineas in a glass jar, corked and then sealed with lead. The jar had been tightly wedged within a hollow stone, and a larger stone had been cemented over the top.

"Very clever. Very well hide," said Jap. "Stone all mossy, no one guess."

In trying to bend his spearhead straight, he had inserted the iron prong in a crevice. The pressure of the spear shaft, as he leaned down on it, acted like a crowbar and pried loose the concealing cemented stone.

"I feel stone move. I say myself, very queer. I look, see cement. I say: this not nature." Working for half an hour, he pried all around the stone and got it free. Underneath was the glass jar.

At last Jap's story was ended. He unrolled the map and flattened it out by re-rolling it the opposite way. Then he thrust it into my hands. "I give you. Here, take," he said. "Jap can't read you Western ABC, but he know. He know this piece paper mean blood and gold." His chunky finger pointed to brown spot at the top right-hand corner. It looked like a blood stain. Then he moved his finger downward until the tip rested on a yellow cross drawn with a crayon.

My eyes were riveted on that yellow cross. Busily my mind's eye fitted the two halves of the map of the *Mary*

LAZ

HMENS
DS

X
X X
X X
X X
X X X
X X X
X X
X

DEDO
DE
MORO

line up

Oak with
sight Laz

find X

N

CONEY
ISLAND

Neddie : his ½

F. together—the half clutched in my hand and the half re-corded in my mind. The lines jibed exactly. This was the missing half; there was no doubt about it.

My first reaction was astonishment—amazement at the placement of the yellow cross. It was at the shore line, so close that a nonswimmer could have scrambled down the rocks and picked up the gold. I was aware of a sickening sense of disappointment. If that cross marked the place where the gold was sunk, then long ago someone had surely found it. Some peasant, some shepherd idly looking for clams must have been dazzled by the blazing treasure flashing beneath the water. No wonder Neddie hadn't been able to find more than three guineas. What fools Fat Jack and Neddie were to sink the treasure so close to shore!

Then I remembered reading that British tars in those days seldom knew how to swim. Now I understood. The two connivers had been thinking of their own interests from the moment they felt those sacks of guineas in their hands—thieves at heart while obeying orders and while their fellow seamen were being attacked by the French. They had been thinking they might come back alone, those two, and grab the money for themselves before the British Government got around to it. And of course the money would have to be near the shore, because neither Fat Jack nor Neddie could swim. Well, someone else had beaten them to it.

My disappointment was so great that I could scarcely bring myself to look at the rest of the map. Of what use was it now? None, unless . . . unless the yellow cross was incorrectly placed. How did it get there? Surely Fat Jack wouldn't have let Neddie get away with a marked half, for then his own half would have been unnecessary. I suspected that Neddie had put the yellow cross there himself, had X'd it in once he got his half to himself, to fortify his memory and put one over on his friend.

Yes, I thought, that must be the origin of the yellow cross. Neddie had placed it in later from memory because he didn't have the bearing.

But *I* had the bearing. I knew it! I turned to study the map—the same pale blue ink, the same rough drawing as Fat Jack's, and at the bottom the legend: "Neddie, his half." But Neddie's half contained a number of crosses made in a darker ink, unlabeled crosses evidently drawn in after the map was made. There seemed no doubt from their positions along the north and east shore of the bay that these crosses marked various places where Neddie had futilely looked for the gold.

As for the bearing, it was instantly clear to me. In the center of the map were the words:

> line up
> oak with
> sight Laz
> find X

Placed side by side in my mind with the legend on Fat Jack's half, the whole read: "Off shr Fr Wd line up shtst gr oak with Atalia sight Laz at 90° to find X." In other words, someone offshore at Frenchmen's Woods could

line up an oak—"shtst gr oak" probably meant the shortest of some grey or great oak trees in the woods—with the
Atalia to the west, and keeping in this line row to the
spot where a sighting of the Lazaretto made a 90-degree
angle to this line. There was X, the gold.

I knew nothing about nautical readings, nothing of
sextants or quadrants; and I know even less today. But
the bearing that Fat Jack and Neddie devised was not
such a clever or ingenious one, and it was easily under-
standable even to a landlubber like me. It was based on
a rule I learned in high school geometry: "Only one perpendicular to a line may be drawn through a given point
outside the line." I quickly saw that the base line was
formed by two points, the Atalia and the oak. The point
through which the perpendicular had to be drawn was
the old quarantine tower. This was a square tower rising
from an abandoned group of buildings across the bay
from Puerto Del Sol. People in town called it the Laza-
reto; it was the compound where during the Middle Ages
and up until the mid-nineteenth century visitors from in-
coming ships were put in quarantine to prevent the
spread of smallpox and plague.

Hoping against hope that Neddie's yellow cross was
misplaced, that it was off the apex of the right angle and
that the treasure had thus escaped him, I decided to test
its accuracy. I took a ruler and protractor from my desk
and quickly drew a dotted line from the quarantine tower
to the yellow cross. Then I measured a right angle with
the protractor at the point of the cross and drew the base
line, extending it to the west edge of the map, the torn

edge. It ran through Frenchmen's Woods; and with a sinking heart I saw that its extension on into the missing half of the map would certainly pass through the Atalia. There was no doubt about it; Neddie's guess had been right. The yellow cross marked the exact place indicated by the bearing. Neddie had had his bearings right after all, even without Fat Jack's half of the map. But there had been no gold.

I threw my ruler aside and looked up at Jap. His face was expectant.

"You understand map, Ron. Gold map, eh?"

"It looks like it, Jap," I said. "But the gold was so close to shore someone's found it long ago. This map is just an old curiosity now."

He beamed. "No more gold, eh? Good." Then he noticed the disappointment on my features, for he added, "You sorry about that?"

He bent over the map and his eyes ran over the rudely-drawn shore line. I could see he was correlating the lines on the map with the rocky shore he knew so well. He put his finger on the small island halfway in from the mouth of the bay. "That Coney Island?" he asked.

"Yes."

He touched the inlet below the Lazaretto. "That Dedo de Moro, yes?"

I nodded.

Jap smiled and jabbed his finger at the yellow cross. "Water very deep here," he said. "Jap know. Good fishing for mero. Ten, twelve yards."

Hope leaped up in me. If the water were deep there, maybe Neddie hadn't been able to get down to the gold. Maybe no one had, and it was still there. "You know that area, Jap?"

"Ya. Very deep some place; very shallow some place. Like cliffs."

"Can you see the bottom from the surface?"

"No, sir. Lots weeds there."

"Maybe the gold is in a deep place," I said. I was alight again with hope.

Jap smiled and patted my arm. "One way find out," he said. "We go there tomorrow. We make sure."

In a moment we were making plans, discussing equipment, guessing just exactly off which rock the cross would lie. I asked: "Are there any big oak trees, old ones, in Frenchmen's Woods?"

"No. Only pine, carob. Little ones. Woods burned down ten years ago."

That meant that the oak tree was gone. I could never take a bearing myself. We would have to trust Neddie's map, trust his golden cross.

We agreed to meet at the dock at seven the next morning. As we talked Jap carefully rolled up the map again and inserted it into the mast of the sampan model. I had made a copy, traced it, marked nothing but the site of the yellow cross.

"Good idea, eh?" said Jap as he slipped the roll of paper into the hollow mast. "Good hide place?" Then he leaned over and whispered in my ear: "*This* what man want rob. Remember? Man with leather hand? This what he after." Jap laughed. "I fool him, eh? Who ever guess nice lady like Miss Valling hide treasure map?"

Something scraped against the door. I sensed it rather than heard it—a noise so light, so soft, like the brushing of a hand against the wall.

In an instant I was at the door. I jerked it open. There in the hallway in the dark crouched on hands and knees was Paco the servant. He looked up at me, blinking, his mouth gaping.

"What are you doing here?" I said.

He held up his hand. There was a scrub brush in it. A bucket of water stood near the wall. "I'm mopping the floor," he said.

"At this time of night? Go on, get out."

Loose-hipped, in his slovenly way, he rose, picked up the bucket, and shuffled off. I was sure he had been listening.

Jap Teaches Me
a Lesson

 It was a perfect morning, the sea like glass and the wind warm and soft. I left a note for my mother telling her I was going out with Jap and might be home late.

He was waiting for me at the dock, standing beside Lobo, his dog, among the henna-colored nets that were spread over the pavement to dry. White gulls flapped and croaked overhead. The little boat gently nudged the quay, tugging politely at its hawser as if anxious to be gone.

Jap and I grinned our greeting and, wordless, set to work stowing the fishing gear in the boat. We never went far without extra spearheads, breathers, and goggles;

there was always the chance that something might break two miles from home and leave us helpless as hens if we didn't have spares. Jap also thought to bring a battery-operated underwater lamp which he had fashioned for himself from a cooky tin, making it watertight with sealing wax.

Though I tried hard to tell myself that the gold had been found at least a century ago and that our expedition was a wild goose chase, I couldn't crush a truant excitement. There was something propitious, infectiously so, in the air—a sense of good luck impending. Everything about me was vivid and sparkling with promise: the flashing water, the China-blue sky, the blossoming hills. And most of all Jap—his bead-like eyes glinting as he worked effortlessly and efficiently. It gave me a sense of joy just to watch him handle the gear. With such a partner I was bound to strike it lucky. He seemed to have lost his distaste for treasure, now that he had decided to hand it over to me if we found it. He was working away, as excited as a boy.

I had been thinking about his generosity during the night and had decided I would force him to take his share. I was younger than he, and youth was worth more than gold. I even thought I'd try to urge the whole of the treasure on him if he weren't too stubborn. In fact, we were the strangest treasure hunters imaginable—both of us eager and ticking away like clocks just for the fun of it, and both of us inwardly planning to give the other the bigger share. We smiled again and again as we stowed the equipment aboard.

Jap had brought along a small sail and a mast. We sometimes used the sail when the wind wasn't too gusty, to spare our backs the wear and tear of rowing, particularly when we had a long distance to cover, as we did today. It was two miles across the bay to the north shore where the yellow cross marked our destination.

Jap was attending to the rigging, I watched, when I heard the pad of cloth shoes beside me. I turned to find Paco at my elbow. Before I could chew him out for skulking around, he handed me a basket. I took it brusquely. He seemed to have a habit of popping up silently when least expected. It was a habit I didn't trust.

"The señora, your mother, sent this for you," he said. "She thought you might need it if you're going to be gone long."

I looked in the basket. There were sandwiches inside, some fruit, and some thermos jugs. I thanked Paco and tucked the basket in the stern, covering it with a piece of oilcloth so the spray wouldn't dampen it. Then I told him curtly to get back to the shop, as mother might need his help.

We shoved off with an oar and in a moment the little three-cornered sail bellied out and we were scudding away. We waved good-bye to Lobo, who barked an excited farewell.

It took us half an hour to make the opposite shore, the boat gliding over the mirror-like sea as smoothly as a swan in spite of its fat hull and square stern. We left a long wake like a pencil line upon the water for a hundred yards behind us. Jap handled the sail and I held the tiller, keeping the boat headed directly for the place marked by the yellow cross.

We anchored fore and aft, exactly above the spot indicated on Neddie's map—as near as we could judge, that is, for we had no proper instruments. The rocky shore lay not ten yards from our port side—heaped-up red rocks with scrub pine rooted in the crannies. It took us a minute or two to put on our masks. Then we prepared to dive.

Our plan was simple. The first dive would be for reconnaissance. We certainly had no harebrained expectations of landing on a sea chest the first time down. Too many years had gone by, enough time for the drift of sand to have covered a grand piano. We were going to scan the bottom, get the lay of the land. Then, depending on what we found, we were going to cover the likeliest section square foot by square foot, using our spears as prodders.

To tell the truth we hardly knew what to look for. Valdez had mentioned strongboxes to me, but that was probably just a manner of speaking. The ceaseless chemical action and rubbing of the water would long ago have disintegrated anything but a lead box. If the gold were here I half expected to find it lying scattered loose, swept into some gulley or crevice, or perhaps into several.

"Ready?" Jap called. We were in the water, clinging to either side of the boat.

I nodded and bent double, kicked myself straight to the bottom. It was a bad dive, for my heart pounded with excitement and my blood racing; it was impossible to hold my lungs full for more than forty-five seconds. But that was long enough for me to see what I wanted.

The sea bottom formed a cup, mottled sand and rocks in the hollow, the lee side rising gently upward until it broke through the surface to form the shore. The sea side was curious, a curious formation—a cliff of jagged rock rising almost sheer from a depth of ten yards up to within a yard of the surface. If formed a nasty reef. I judged the depth of the cup at its deepest point to be about twelve yards. From rim to rim—that is, from the shore to the top of the reef—it must have measured forty yards.

It struck me at once as I hovered down there, peering rapidly this way and that, that Fat Jack and Neddie had hit by chance on a natural container. It almost seemed as if the spot had been selected by plan, though I knew it couldn't have been. The gold could never have been swept out to sea, for the semi-circular reef wall would have damned in anything that didn't float. The money was either underneath the sand or it wasn't here at all, I thought. Our search was going to be simpler than we had expected.

Back at the surface Jap's face blinked at me. "Easy, eh?" he said, voicing my own thought.

"Yes."

"You take that side," he pointed toward the sea. "I take this."

We separated. I swam a few strokes outward until I was above the reef. Then I dived, descending down the side of the sheer rock. Clinging to an outcropping to give myself leverage, I jammed my spear into the sand at the base of the cliff. It touched nothing. Pulling it out, I thrust it in again a few inches to the left. Again I withdrew it and jabbed again, a few more inches to the left. Starting there at the base of the cliff, I planned to cover the bottom, bit by bit, working my way inward to the center of the hollow. I caught sight of Jap from time to time, murky and looming larger than life, as everything does under the sea, magnified as it is by the prismatic effect of the moving water. He was some twenty yards away from me, exploring the shore side, working his way toward me. Occasionally we broke surface at the same time; then we would halloo to each other.

"Hit anything?" I would call.

"Not yet." And in a second he had ducked his head under, his feet flashed above the surface, and he had disappeared into the depths.

It was exhausting work to stick the spear into the sand —that shifting, bottomless sand. Sometimes I lost my bearings, as one does under water, and felt I was poking again and again over the same area. My arms ached. Stab in the spear, twist it, pull it out, come up for air. And then down again. My lungs felt close to bursting, and sometimes the pressure on my temples was like a steel vise. The bamboo spear seemed so inadequate a tool, so thin and fragile. I could only probe an area five inches square each time, no matter how roughly I twisted and shoved the spear back and forth.

We worked for more than an hour without the slightest result, not even a sardine can. I was fairly winded. Each dive required greater and greater effort. It's no child's play to buck the pressure at ten yards. My head was throbbing. And I began to see what a fool's errand we had come on. A hundred and fifty years of ceaseless motion could have covered the gold under ten feet of sand. Small as the hollow was in the vastness of the sea bottom, it enclosed some fifteen hundred square yards. Months would be needed simply to examine it in the hit-or-miss way we were going; even so, we were only pricking the sand.

I was treading water slowly, gulping in big draughts of air, preparing to go down again, when Jap burst through the surface and signaled me. For a moment I thought he might have struck something. But he was only calling a halt, a breathing space. We swam to shore and climbed out, throwing ourselves panting on the sun-baked rocks. I lay there face down, too tired to speak, hugging the hot rocks, trying to get rid of the chill which had penetrated to my marrow.

I don't know how long I lay there, half numb, when I heard a little exclamation from Jap. He sat up with a jerk and began to feel around over the rocks with the flat of his hand.

"Ron. Listen," he said. Bone-tired as I was, I sat up and cocked my head. I heard a hollow, sucking noise— a deep, growling that seemed to come from beneath us. The sound was unmistakable; it was the sound of heaving water echoing within the earth.

Jap grasped my hand and pressed it against the rock he had been lying on. I felt a rhythmic trembling faint as a pulse beat.

Jap patted the rock. "Cave here. Cave under us, right here. Water in it."

I agreed. I couldn't understand his sudden interest. The coast was pocked with little caves and big ones, worn by the action of the waves against the soft sandstone that formed much of the shore line.

Jap hopped spryly to his feet and strapped on his goggles. He seemed as fresh as he had been that morning. I started to rise too, but he motioned me to stay where I was. "You rest," he said. "Jap find cave door. Maybe important. Maybe just fun."

Glad of the chance to stretch out again, I marveled at his stamina and thought to myself that if Jap's idea of fun was to start diving again, it wasn't mine. In a moment he had slipped into the water. Resting my head on my elbow, I watched him for a while as he made his way west along the shore line, diving, coming up for air, diving again. He was such an expert swimmer that he didn't make a splash, not a sound nor a bit of churned-up foam, when he went down. It was curious to watch him as he disappeared silently in one spot only to pop back again some twenty or thirty feet distant just as silently. It was a guessing game to keep track of him.

I could see that he was examining the rocks beneath the shore line, looking for a hole, an opening which would lead into the cave. Pretty soon the surface around him was bobbing with hanks of seaweed which he had pulled out in his efforts to uncover the opening.

He stayed in the water a long time. I lay back and closed my eyes. I was warm now; the tingling numbness had gone from my fingers. But I was discouraged. I had given up all hope of gold and was thinking about getting home. I was hungry. Warm as the rocks were, they were hard. I longed to lean back in my wicker chair under the banana tree in our patio and read about a gold hunt that had turned out better than ours.

I was lost in such fancies when Jap, panting and spewing water like a dolphin, climbed out on the rock beside me. Icy drops showered over me as he shook the hair out of his eyes. There was a look of triumph in his grin.

"Jap find cave door. Two yards under. Over there." He indicated a spot some hundred yards to the west.

I sat up and laughed. Jap was a sight to see—his brown, muscular body agleam with water drops, his black hair plastered flat like a skullcap. His teeth were chattering; he was shaking and shivering all over and slapping his sides to get warm.

"Come and sit down," I said. "Stretch out on the rocks. They're hot as an oven."

"No, No," he said, hopping about and stamping his feet. "Listen, Ron, listen." He put his finger to his forehead. "Jap get idea. Jap not smart with books, but very smart with nature. You know what? You remember I hear water noise under here, remember?"

"Yes."

"I say myself: cave under here. Then I think: Jap, you idiot, cave very near gold place. Then I say myself: what make cave? Water make cave. Water move, water push. Water always push same place, always same place, same way. Then I think: if water push cave into rock, maybe water push gold into cave? Then I say: find cave, find gold. What you think, Ron?"

I was smiling. To tell the truth, the idea seemed a pretty wild guess, and I hardly listened. Jap looked so funny and solemn as he talked.

He lay out flat on the rocks. I sat next to him, and only then did I give any thought to what he had just said. The more I thought, the more excited I got. There was a possibility, a far chance.

"Jap," I said, "down there at the mouth of the cave did you feel a strong current? A current rushing inwards, into the cave opening?"

"You bet. Strong as kick in pants," he said. "Almost kick me right in."

That was good. That meant something. A current would have to be strong to sweep in some three hundred pounds of gold coin.

"Could you see inside, Jap?"

"No see. Lots of weeds there."

"Can we get into the cave, do you think, Jap?"

"We see. Maybe. Jap tired now." And he closed his eyes. In a moment he was actually asleep, breathing deeply and evenly. Eaten up with impatience, I decided to try to get into the cave myself. I put on my goggles and slipped silently into the water.

Swimming leisurely to the west, keeping on the surface with my goggled face in the water, I followed the shore line. It was easy to keep on Jap's trail, for he had ripped away seaweed at various places along the rocks.

In a few minutes I spotted the cave mouth—a dark,

angular hole about four feet in diameter, big enough to
swim through and follow along for quite a distance, if one
could be sure of getting air farther in. It was even big
enough to turn around in. If . . . if only the passage
were short and the cave opened up inside . . .

I dived. Shafts of sunlight fell aslant through the water
and into the cave opening, lighting it for a distance of five
feet inside. Beyond that I could see nothing—a velvety
blackness. I felt around with my spear, trying to judge
whether the ceiling of the cave seemed to go upward. It
did.

I came up for a mouthful of air, keeping my eyes
closed so that once back down again I could see better in
the dark. Then, back again, peering intently into the
black, water-filled opening, I thought I could discern a
definite and continuing rise in the ceiling. As the cave
penetrated the rock, it widened. I was sure of it.

I thrust my head and shoulders into the cave and,
stretching my arm as far forward as I could, I felt the cave
floor with the spear. It slanted downwards. That was luck,
for a cave with a floor inclining toward the sea couldn't
have held the gold. It would have washed back out again.

I was excited now. I could feel the forces of the current
Jap talked about. It seemed to suck me into the black
hole. I had to brace myself against it.

Filling my lungs again at the surface I dived for the
third time and, hovering at the cave entrance, I let myself
be forced inward by the current. I wanted to test the
strength of the current. Also I felt a curious desire to go
farther and farther in. In a couple of seconds my whole

body was deep within the cave passage. Everything was inky black. Holding my spear ahead of me, I felt along the ceiling as I let myself be carried swiftly forward. The spear touched nothing. That must mean that the ceiling had suddenly risen—higher than the length of my spear.

My lungs were strong and full, but I knew that I had still to go out, turn around, and swim five strokes out of the passage and two more strokes to the surface. I decided to risk surfacing here inside the cave. Maybe my head would emerge into air. I kicked myself upward and smashed against stone, a blow that made me see stars. The water still reached the cave ceiling.

That blow frightened me, put me off balance. It wasn't the shock of the blow so much as the shock of finding that I had misjudged. It doesn't do to misjudge under water, for you have no minutes to spare, no time to reconsider, just a couple of minutes between you and death by drowning.

I felt suddenly weak and panicky. I was terribly afraid I had come inside too far, and fought down an irresistible urge to open my mouth. My lungs were aching for air. I had lost time, precious time, when dazed by the blow.

But my mind clicked on logically. I kept warning myself not to lose my nerve or it would be all up with me. I doubled up and turned a somersault until I was heading outward again. Ahead I could see the opening, shining green. Five strong kicks and I was through it. Two more and my head shot out above the surface. I opened my mouth and gulped in the air.

Then something pulled me under. Something soft and

elastic was clasping my left foot around the ankle. I lost my head. There were octopuses in these waters, hundreds of them. Most were small, but the fisherman told tales of giant ones, big enough to strangle a man.

I was sure that one of these monsters had grabbed me. The steadiness of his pull on my leg was stronger than all my violent efforts to kick myself free. My blood began to pound with panic.

I got to the surface again and screamed Jap's name, but my scream was choked off as I swallowed water and sank again. I began to kick hysterically at the thing that was clasping my foot. It swayed, but it didn't let go. I strained to the surface again, gasped air and was tugged under. I dared not look down to see what it was that held me. I was afraid the sight might make me lose my head altogether. I fought blindly, kicking as hard as I could, sometimes bobbing up for air, only to be tugged under again.

Then Jap was beside me. I dug my fingers into his shoulder. "Left foot," I gasped. He took out his knife and dived.

Though panic was wild in me, I ceased kicking so that Jap could see to cut me loose. Holding my breath, I let the thing pull me under. I felt Jap's hand brush against my leg. Then I was free.

I swam for shore and scrambled out, not caring that I scratched myself on the jagged points of the rocks. A few moments later Jap was beside me. He was furious. "You all right?" he asked.

I nodded. I was too breathless to speak.

With a grunt he threw the spear he carried onto the

rocks and spat out one word: "Fool!" I saw that the rubber loop on the spear handle was cut in two. My heart trembled; what had happened to *my* spear? Then everything was clear to me. *This* was my spear. I must have dropped it when I struck my head. And the loop had somehow become tangled around my left foot. As I had surfaced, the spearhead had hooked under a rock. It had been the elastic of my own spear tugging me under. I was ready to cry with shame.

"What you go out for alone?" asked Jap angrily. "Don't Jap say hundred times: never go alone? But Ron big fisherman now. Big fellow. Want show off how big. Ha! The sea, she know what do with show-off. You fool. Fool way to die. Yes sir, show-off is fool way to die."

I couldn't look at him. I turned my head away.

"All right, boy," said Jap after a while and in a kindlier tone. "You scared, yes? You scared good?"

"Yes."

"That good. Now you smart. Now you smarter."

There was a long silence. I had got my breath back, but I was still suffering from remorse. Jap said: "You tired?"

"I don't know. I'm still shaking a little, but I think it's just fright. What a dope I was!"

"You bet," said Jap cheerfully. Then: "We go in cave now."

I looked at him, startled. I wasn't anxious to go down there again.

"Best way when scared," said Jap. "Go down again. Right away."

Telling me to wait where I was, he swam out to the boat. After hauling up the anchors, he rowed west until he was a few yards out from where I sat. He threw out the anchors fore and aft, securing the boat so it wouldn't wash against the rocks. Then he slipped his goggles down from his forehead. (Out of the water he wore them pushed up like a granny's reading glasses.) He hung the underwater lamp around his neck and swam over to me.

"Come on," he called. "We find gold now, easy." He was smiling; he was thinking he had spoken too harshly to me.

Still feeling shaky, I buckled on my mask and let myself down into the water.

5

The Red Cave

Jap said he would go in first. I was to wait for him at the mouth of the cave. He instructed me to pick up a fair-sized stone once I was down. It would keep me ballasted and spare my strength. Also, it would keep me right side up—not an easy task underwater in the path of a two-knot current.

I had scarcely crouched down and heaved a stone between my knees when Jap disappeared into the opening. I could distinguish his silhouette far inside, behind the lantern which hung from his neck, its light beaming ahead. He looked small and distant, almost swallowed up in the dim, shadowy undulations of the water. But in a moment he had flipped around and was swimming back. We surfaced together.

"Plenty big cave," he said excitedly.

"Did you reach the cavern?"

He nodded vigorously several times. "Big as house," he said. Then he asked me if I thought I could swim twenty yards along the passage. The cavern opened up after twenty yards, he said, and there I could surface for air.

Though I felt pretty humble about my abilities now, I nodded. "Yes, I think I can swim it."

"Current carry you in," said Jap. "But you got fight it coming out. You feel all right?"

"Yes."

Without another word he went down and I followed. He entered in front of me, lighting the way. I didn't see much, just a murky brown bottom beneath me—very close at first, close enough to reach down and touch, and then deepening. I was concentrating on getting through the passage as fast as I could, trying to take advantage of the current pushing me along, but fighting, too, not to let it get control of me and scrape me against the rocky sides of the passage. I had plenty of breath left when in less than a minute I saw Jap surface ahead of me. I kicked myself up and found myself swimming inside a grotto, with my head above water at last.

I had never seen such a place in my life; I had never been in a sea cave before. The ceiling arched above me like a groined roof—ten feet or more above the water level. Hundreds of stalactites, slender as pencils, crystalline white and glittering like snow, hung from it. They looked prickly, sharp as icicles, yet with a powdery quality as if brushed over with new fallen snow. The walls of the cave were rippled, satiny—as if varnished with shellac and colored from a paint pot.

Jap, treading water ahead of me, turned the beam of his lantern upward. The light cast great, moving shadows over everything. Reflected light from the water surface danced in brilliant points over the walls and ceiling, darting like gunfire and giving the eerie impression that the whole place was moving.

"How you like?" Jap called, his voice bouncing from wall to wall.

"Pretty."

"Very pretty. Like birthday cake," shouted Jap. Again his voice rumbled and echoed. The word "cake" was repeated and repeated, growing fuzzier until at last it died away in the slap, slap of the water.

Jap hooked his lamp over a rock and we both swam leisurely around, exploring our cave and enjoying ourselves like two children on a holiday. As my eyes became used to the dim, wavering light I saw that the cavern was actually quite small, just a pocket in the rocks no bigger than a ballroom, I judged. It was roughly oblong in shape, the farthest point inward being a sort of niche. That was evidently where the current was at work, eating away the sandstone. To the right the wall was seamed with fissures, and the water gurgled in and out of them making a rhythmic noise that echoed with a muffled beat. Evidently the fissures were deep, perhaps running for dozens of yards through the earth, parallel to the surface. It must have been above one of these fissures that Jap first heard the sounds which led him to find the cave.

Jap hallooed to me and climbed out on a rock. As I pulled myself up beside him he laughed. "Pretty good place for treasure, eh, Ron? Spooky."

I had completely forgotten about the gold.

"If gold in here," said Jap, "same as in you pocket." He was enjoying himself, craning his neck to stare at the ceiling formations, running his stocky fingers up and down the damp-slick walls.

I picked up the lantern and beamed it into the water, trying to light up the bottom.

I almost dropped the lamp. The bottom was red, blood red. I glanced at my body, half expecting to see red stains on my skin. Somehow, the bloody color made me shudder. I began to feel an anxiety to get out into the sunlight.

"Jap," I said, "am I crazy? The water is red."

"Red weeds."

Then I understood. The red algae I had noticed outside at certain spots along the rocks grew here in profusion, blossoming red in the darkness. I remembered Jap's prediction that Neddie's map meant blood and gold and felt a chill as if a cold wind had touched the nape of my neck.

"Let's get out," I said.

"One minute. I look at bottom." Having the lamp around his neck he slipped into the water. Unexpectedly I found myself thrust into darkness. The light was far beneath the water with Jap, its beams cast downward. And their faint reflections, red and veiled, only made the darkness above more ghostly. I watched Jap kicking himself around the bottom, his body glowing palely. He looked like some mythical sea creature swimming in a pool of blood—like someone I had never known. I felt utterly alone. Gradually, stealthily, a sense of suffocation took hold of me. I felt trapped within this bubble of air deep under the earth's crust. My hands and feet began to tingle with the cold. Only then did I realize that the cave was clammy and dark, as cold as an icebox. Indeed, I felt as if I were locked inside a box, slowly freezing to death.

I jumped to my feet. The atmosphere was beginning to unnerve me. I edged my way toward the exit passage—or toward the place where I thought it was. For it was under the water, invisible to me. By concentrating on the slippery footing I warded off my fears—at least I kept them under control. But I was aware of an intense longing to see the sky again, to feel the limitless space of the sea around me and to breathe the fresh, salty air.

Clinging to the damp rocks I made my way as fast as I could. In every crevice my hands seemed to touch soft, slimy moving things. It took all my will power not to let go with a shudder. Gradually, in that intense darkness, I became aware of the never-ending murmur and gurgle of the water—a sound which, magnified by my strained senses, seemed loud and menacing. It seemed to drum at me from all sides, closing in on me just as the walls seemed to close in. Sweat broke out all over my body.

Fighting down a rising panic, I sat down. I watched the light, waiting, waiting for it to rise up to me. It seemed to me that Jap had been under an hour. I wondered with a stab of horror if he were trapped below. But in a moment there was his face crinkled in a grin and bobbing like a cork over the water. I could have embraced him. With him came his blessed light, chasing away the shadows and the gloom.

He looked anxiously toward the rock where he had left me.

"I'm here, over here," I called.

He turned and swam over, climbing up beside me. "Where you go? You try take walk in here, Ron?"

"Well," I said, trying to make my voice casual, "I thought I'd edge over toward the exit, you know, have more breath to make the trip out against the current."

He looked at me in astonishment. "You crazy. You go wrong way. Look. This is far point in."

He was right. In my panic I had mixed up the directions. Instead of going toward the exit I had come inward until now I was seated in the niche that formed the deepest point of the cave. It was the second serious error in judgment I'd made that morning. My face must have paled, for Jap asked: "You want go now?"

"Yes."

"Good." Then to show that he understood my fears and sympathized with them he said: "Pretty spooky here. Anyway, cave no good for gold. We go." He clucked his tongue. "No gold. Bottom all rock. All rock with red weed. Very short weed like goat hair. No hide place. No gold."

I was relieved; I would never have to enter this place again. Hurrying, I put on my mask and waited for Jap.

He was reaching down to pick up the lantern when he stopped stock still. He gripped my hand and pointed straight down, straight at the lantern.

There was the British gold.

The gold was glinting up at us with a hundred prickles of dull yellow light, winking beneath the lantern's base. The lantern was sitting on top of it, on top of a pool of guineas, just like the ones Jap had found in Neddie's glass jar. They were spread out as neat and pretty as you please, lying in the hollow of the rock which held them as if it were a basket.

I could do nothing but stare. I had been sitting on top of them.

Jap let out a whoop, and the next thing I knew he had taken a backward somersault into the water, whooping for joy. His face appeared on the surface in an instant. He was laughing like a fool. "What you think, Ron? We buy you mama nice present, eh?"

I knelt down and touched the guineas. I half expected to find that they were a mirage. But they were real, hard and slimy just like the rocks. I tried to dig my hand into them, to pick some up. But I couldn't. They were stuck fast, calcified to the rock and to each other. With a shock I realized that the action of the sea had cemented them fast where they lay. I scratched at one of the top ones, tearing my fingernail. It wouldn't budge.

Jap climbed out beside me. "Well, let's go," he said. "Fill you pocket. You rich, boy."

I was staring down at the guineas. The strains of that

eventful day were telling on me at last. I felt weak and shaky, gripped by an impulse to burst into wild laughter.

I could see exactly what had occurred. It was as plain as day. A long time ago, perhaps just a year or two after our thieving lads from the *Mary F.* had sunk the strongbox of British gold in the hollow outside the cave, a high sea had pried it loose. Then the current had picked it up and swept the gold into the cave and deposited it here—here in the obvious place against the back wall at the spot where the current wore away the rock bit by bit, performing its secret erosion in the depths of the sea. The strongbox had become wedged immovably in the hollow of the rock. With the years the box had disintegrated, all except its steel bands. There they were like gaunt ribs, rusted and crumbled. And the gold in the course of the decades had been claimed by the earth, cemented fast to the rock within which it lay. I could see now the little shells and skeletons of sea worms curling and winding among the guineas, forming a natural lime concrete. The gold was one with the rock, united again to the earth from which it had been wrested. Young as I was, the fitness of this destiny struck me, and the irony of it. There the gold lay, tempting, seductive—and unobtainable. I tried to laugh.

Jap looked at me queerly. I must have sounded strange. My laugh was almost a croak.

"Ron. Fill you pocket. We go," he said.

"I can't pick it up, Jap. You go ahead and try," I said.

He shot his hand down and met with the solid mass.

He looked up, puzzled; he tried again. Then he burst into a raucous laugh. "Good joke! Good joke!" he shouted. "What you think about that?"

"Come on," I said. "Let's get out of this place. It gives me the creeps."

Back in the boat we lay about in the sun to dry, not speaking, each busy with his own thoughts. After a while I opened the lunch basket that mother had sent along. Jap continued to chuckle to himself as we started in on the sandwiches. Every once in a while he would slap his knee and give out a short hoot of a laugh. He thought it a good joke. As for me, I didn't know what to think. I was too tired to care very much. We ate in silence.

Jap said: "I thirsty. What you got there?"

I opened one of the thermos jugs and sniffed at it. Hot cocoa. Good Lord, my mother would never get over thinking of me as a child. "This one's for me," I said. Then I fished around for the other thermos and took out the cork. It was red wine. I handed it to Jap, who tilted the jug back and drank deep.

Not ten minutes later, as I was collecting the bits of garbage—fruit peeling and paper—preparing to sink them with a stone, I happened to look over at Jap and saw him doubled up. His head was between his knees. There was something unnatural, strained about the way he was bent over. I called his name. He didn't answer.

I let go of the packet of garbage and sprawled over to him, nearly capsizing the boat and then righting it with such a jerk that I was thrown to my knees.

"Hey, Jap!" I knelt before him. He groaned and remained bent over. His arms were crossed over his abdomen; he was hugging himself as if in great pain.

"Jap, what happened?" I said. Then as he didn't answer I jerked his head up—not very gently, I'm afraid—and began slapping and rubbing his cheeks. I was half wild with fear. I didn't know what to do. What had happened? A heart attack? A cramp? His lips were bluish; his eyes rolled back. A white foam was at the corners of his mouth.

I grabbed up an old sun hat and dipped up some water, sloshing it into Jap's face, flinging it at him. He began to cough as the water went up his nose and into his mouth.

"What's the matter with you?" I shouted. I was pulling and pummelling him as if I could beat him into consciousness. Sweat was beaded along his brows and on his upper lip.

He bent double again with a spasm and began to retch with great racking heaves and sobs as if he were coughing up his insides.

When it was over he lifted his head and looked at me with deep shadowy eyes, so different from his usual glance. His face was like a sheet of white paper. But he was better; I sensed it in the way he shook his head is if to clear it. I was so relieved I could have cried.

I reached over for the jug of wine and tried to pour a little down him. Weak as he was he thrust the jug aside and turned his head away with a grimace. "No, no. More sea water."

Using the hat as a dipper I gave him sea water. He

must have swallowed half a pint and then began at once to vomit again, half slumping to the bottom of the boat. After a while he lay back, resting his head against the gunwale, and closed his eyes. His breath was jerky and rapid; then gradually it grew even and regular. He smiled at me feebly.

Afraid that he might have another attack, I watched him closely, wiping his forehead and neck with a damp rag. He opened his eyes and said: "Bad wine."

"Are you all right, Jap?" I said, scarcely listening to his words. "Are you all right?"

He smiled.

"You just lie there, Jap. I'll get you back. We'll get a doctor."

"Wine taste funny. Maybe poison," he said. He lay back and almost instantly fell into a doze of exhaustion. I sat listening to his breathing for some time. It remained even and steady. His face had regained its burnished color and though his lips were puckered and dry they were relaxed. I spread a tarpaulin over him and took up the oars.

I didn't dare hoist the sail; I didn't know anything about sailing. So I rowed, exhausted as I was.

I've never crossed a longer two miles in my life. Jap's boat was small as fishing boats go, but it was ten feet from stem to stern—a hefty size for a rowboat, and built all wrong. The oars were seven feet long, and heavy—made of chestnut wood. I wasn't halfway home before my back was breaking and my hands swelling with broken blisters.

Sometimes it seemed to me I was making no progress at all. And the whole time I watched the sleeping Jap, alert to his every murmur and move, ready to leap toward him if I saw any signs of pain. His face remained smooth and peaceful.

I dipped the heavy oars in, pulled back, lifted them, dipped them in again—how many hundreds of times I don't know. I tried to keep the stern in line with the light-house, for, of course, I was facing aft and couldn't see where I was going without truning around in my seat. It wasn't an easy job. And my mind kept drifting off to other things, stuffed as it was to overflowing with the day's happenings, weary and dulled with too much strain and emotion. I found my thoughts constantly veering off to the gold, to the eerie red cave, and most of all to Jap's sudden attack.

For the first time I considered Jap's words: "Wine . . . poison." What had he meant by them? Could the wine actually have been poisoned? I didn't see how. My mother must have filled the thermos herself, and it was the wine she drank with her meals at home—the ordinary from Gordo's gin shop.

Toward the last I was bucking the evening current, fighting the small drift seaward that always set in about sundown. The sun was blazing behind the hills. I had been almost three hours at the oars. By that time I had become an automation, thinking nothing. My hands were bleeding, but I felt no pain when at last I docked and moored the little boat at the quay of Puerto Del Sol.

The faithful Lobo was there and jumped into the boat. He seemed distraught at the sight of the sleeping Jap and bounded over to lick his face.

I shook Jap gently awake. He was rested, and when I suggested that I go for a doctor he shook his head. He had a mortal fear of doctors, was afraid one might cut him open when his resistance was low.

I was too tired to argue with him, and we set off for his house. I held onto his arm, but he didn't need my support now. He was all right. Whatever had poisoned him had been retched up out of his system. He didn't even want to go to bed, so I left him seated in his rattan chair by the window. The dog, Lobo, was beside him, licking his hand. As I turned to go, Jap said simply: "Good boy, Ron. Jap thank you."

"Are you sure you're all right now?"

"Yes. All right now. But I poisoned. That I sure. Man with leather hand, he do it. Jap sure about that."

"Well, get a good sleep. Good-bye."

6

Gordo of the Gin Shop

Ⓥ *I tried to hide my raw palms from mother when* I got home, but she caught me painting them with iodine. Exclaiming and scolding, she sat me down on a stool and bustled about with warm water, absorbent cotton, bandages and salves—a regular pharmacy of things. All the while she gave me a lecture. I kept protesting that I didn't need such fussing over, but I was glad of it. And the lecture was small payment to make for Jap's life. Anyway, my mother's bark was worse than her bite.

"Now you just listen to me, young man. You're not too old to get paddled, let me tell you. And I'm the one to do it, don't think I'm not. You're not going out on any

85

more of these trips if I catch you coming back again with hands like these. Look at yourself. You'll be lucky if you don't get a good case of septic poisoning. . . ." And on she went until she finished up with a snap: "Now explain yourself, son."

"Mother, I told you. I had to row back. The sail . . . the wind wasn't right for the sail."

"And where was Mr. Jap? Why couldn't he help?"

"He was sick. He had an attack."

"What do you mean an attack? An attack of what?"

"I don't know. But he was very sick. He wasn't able to row."

She paused, thinking of Jap. "Poor man. Where is he? Perhaps I'd better get the doctor for him."

"No, he's all right now. He's home."

"Well, what happened to him? I don't understand."

"He began to vomit, mother. All of a sudden. He was awfully weak, cramps or something."

She clucked her tongue sympathetically. "Why didn't you give him a little of the wine? It calms an upset stomach."

"He had some wine. That's what made him sick. He thinks the wine was poisoned."

"Poisoned? Our wine? Fiddlesticks! I keep it tightly corked. Nothing could have got inside the demijohn." She finished bandaging my hands and began to put away the gauze and adhesive tape. She repeated: "Our wine spoiled? Where is that thermos?"

I told her I had put the basket in the kitchen. She left the room and brought it back. She had the stopper out of the thermos and was sniffing at it. "Smells all right to me," she said. She went to the sideboard and got a glass. "I'll just have a taste to see."

I jumped up. "Don't, mother."

The agitation in my voice made her pause. "Why, I'm sure it's all nonsense," she said.

"Please don't, mother. Don't take the chance. Jap was really sick."

She smiled. "Well, all right. But I'm sure there's nothing wrong with it. Here . . ." she said brightly, reaching for a saucer from the sideboard. "I'll give some to the cat. She likes wine, but I'm sure she won't touch it if it doesn't smell right to her."

We poured a saucer full and called the cat. She came bounding in from the patio, went up to the saucer, sniffed at it and looked up at mother. We waited. The cat circled the saucer and approached it from the other side. At last she turned away with an aggrieved look mewing plaintively.

Mother looked at me astonished. "Why, she won't touch it." Then with a firm gesture mother corked the thermos, set it on the table, and left the room. In an instant she was back with her hat and coat on.

"I'm going down to that fat man who sold me this, and I'm going to give him a piece of my mind," she snapped. She was collecting her market basket and her purse, all the while talking. "Poisoning decent people. He ought to be jailed. Probably put some cheap chemical in his wine, some poisonous coloring matter. I've half a mind to report this to the police. People like that are a menace. I always thought that Gordo might be a fake with his big talk about honor and all that."

Mother was not to be dissuaded. She was a quiet, orderly woman as a rule, even a bit shy. But when she met up with injustice or bad faith there was no stopping her.

"I'm coming with you," I said.

"You don't need to, son," she said. "I know you get embarrassed when I go off the handle like this. But I wouldn't sleep a wink tonight if I didn't get this off my chest. And I'm not ashamed to tell off that bully. I may be only a woman, but someone's got to speak up."

She marched down the street like a soldier, her face stern beneath the brim of her little black hat, her gloved hands clutching the thermos. I trailed along beside her, afraid they would mock her at Gordo's gin shop. It wasn't a place for a lady to enter after seven, when the workers came in for their evening cups of gin.

There were four men hanging around drinking when mother opened the door and stepped briskly up to the bar, looking every inch the lady. Her eyes were flashing. I was proud of her. At the same time I was dreading the scene she was about to cause. I was sure Gordo would deny everything.

Gordo, florid and sweaty, was behind the bar. He smiled as she entered and ducked his chin in greeting. He rather liked mother; she never niggled.

Mother answered him with a chilly stare. She tapped the thermos on the counter and began at once to lay down the law. She was speaking English, of course, not one word of which Gordo understood. But her tone was unmistakable. Gordo looked abashed. The others in the room gathered around.

"I don't understand you, señora," Gordo said when mother paused.

This didn't deter her. She started in again. To illustrate her words she uncorked the thermos and pointed to its contents. "There. That's what you sold me, sir. I'm not afraid to tell you that if I reported this you would be locked up. Don't pretend you don't know anything about it. A man was nearly killed today drinking this stuff. Now I want an explanation, and I insist you destroy the barrel or whatever it is that this came from. Your shop ought to be shut down."

Gordo scratched his head. He had picked up the thermos and was holding it in one hand, completely baffled.

Mother had at last ceased. "You tell him what I said, Ron," she said. I stepped forward.

"What's the matter, son?" Gordo asked me. "Doesn't your mother like the wine? She's a good customer. I'll give you another kind if this isn't to her liking."

"We think the wine has been poisoned," I said calmly enough. It was the wrong thing to say. Gordo swelled up like an adder and began sputtering. Hastily I went on: "Jap, the spear fisherman, drank some today and got deathly sick."

"Not on *my* wine!" said Gordo, outraged. He lifted the thermos, smelled it. Then he poured a little wine into his palm and licked it off. He closed his eyes and ran his tongue around inside his cheek. "Yes, this is my wine," he said. "My wine never hurt a month-old baby. It's the pure grape. Your friend got sick on something else."

Trying to mollify him, I said: "Well, perhaps. But I think we should take it to the pharmacist. Maybe he can analyze it and tell what's in it."

"The pharmacist! That scoundrel. He knows nothing about wine." Gordo was growing heated. The men in the room were smiling. Gordo bent over the counter and addressed himself to mother. He spoke very earnestly.

"Señora, I swear on the tears of the Virgin that I have never put anything in my wine. You have wounded me. You have libeled me—me, an honorable man. My grandfather was a wine seller, and his father before him. We are proud of our profession. Never have I received such an insult." His big, bleary eyes were peering into mother's. I believed him. Even mother was wavering.

"What does he say, Ron?" she asked.

I didn't have time to answer, for Gordo with a melodramatic sigh lifted up the thermos and drank it all down, what remained of the entire quart. I watched him, horrified.

"There," he said, wiping his mouth with the back of his hand. "That will prove my honor. That sneaky little Japanese has been trying to destroy my reputation. Just let me catch him and I'll wring his neck."

Mother and I continued to stare, waiting for Gordo to cramp up with pain. But he went calmly about pouring a drink for a new customer who had just entered.

"Let's go," I said.

Mother beckoned Gordo. "Sir, I want to tell you I am

satisfied. You have proved your integrity. Please accept my apologies." I translated this and Gordo nodded pleasantly.

We were at the door; I had opened it for mother when from behind us someone bellowed like a bull. I spun around. There was Gordo bent over, clutching his fat belly, his face contorted with pain and surprise. He had knocked off a row of wine glasses, which clattered and bounced all over the room.

Gordo was cut from different cloth than Jap. He roared and thrashed about. It was horrible to see him; at the same time it was slightly funny. People came pouring into the gin shop. Soon a milling crowd of men had stretched Gordo out on his own bar top. Luckily, the doctor lived a few doors down and he came as soon as he heard the commotion.

Mother wanted to stay and help; she felt responsible. But it wasn't the kind of place for a lady. The doctor was already administering an antidote and Gordo was belching up the wine. I thought we had better go home.

As we walked along, mother berated herself. "It's all my fault," she said. "But how could I know he would drink it?"

"You were ready to drink it yourself," I said.

"Why so I was," she said absently-mindedly.

I was thinking. I believed Gordo; he certainly hadn't put anything in the wine or he wouldn't have been so ready to make the test on himself. But he had proved *one* thing: the wine was poisoned. At least the wine in the thermos was. Who had had access to it?

"Mother," I said, "when we get home we'll offer the cat some wine from the main jug, the jug from which you filled the thermos."

"Yes. All right," she said, then added, "but it isn't poisoned. I had a glass this afternoon. I was feeling a bit under the weather. It perked me right up."

"Then someone must have poisoned the thermos. Did you fill it yourself?"

"Yes." I could see she was more concerned than she appeared. Suddenly she looked very tired and worn. I put my arm around her, but she made no response. "Ron," she said in a low, tired voice, "I don't feel easy. I don't feel safe after this."

Was she losing heart again? I pressed my arm tighter about her. "Don't worry. It's just some silly accident, I'm sure."

She shook her head. "Oh Ron, I feel so discouraged all of a sudden." She was wringing her hands around the handle of her purse. Then almostly inaudibly, as if speaking to herself, she said, "I feel helpless without your father, so helpless." My heart sank.

"I'm here, mother," I said quietly. Then more cheerfully, "I'm sure we'll find out that it was an accident. Paco probably dipped his finger in the thermos and infected the wine with some filth or other."

"Paco?" she said. "Why should Paco want to poison Mr. Jap?"

I had been debating this very point with myself and meant to have it out with Paco as soon as we got home.

I remembered only too well that he had been listening outside the door. He must have learned about the map. But why poison Jap? Perhaps to get him out of the way. Perhaps Paco thought the poison would work underwater and thus be undiscovered, for Jap certainly would have been drowned if he had taken any wine before diving.

"Paco?" mother said again. "But I didn't give the lunch basket to Paco. I gave it to Mr. Valdez."

To Valdez!

"Mother," I said, "you get on back to the Kansas City. I'm going to see Mr. Valdez." Before she could protest I squeezed her hand and ran off.

Valdez lived in the main plaza, a good ten-minute walk. As I hurried along I speculated, racking my brains to solve the curious fact of the poisoned thermos. Mother had given the basket to Valdez. Why hadn't he brought it to the dock? Perhaps he'd been busy. He had run into Paco and had handed it over, a perfectly logical thing. But had he tampered with it first? Or had Paco? Or were they in partnership? Had Paco told Valdez about Neddie's half of the map? Suddenly I remembered that it was Valdez who had sent Paco to us the year before, when we first arrived. This struck me as significant. And Valdez was interested in the British gold; he suspected Jap of withholding information from him.

The nearer I came to Valdez's house the more uneasy I became. What was I going to ask him? He was a man of great composure and experience; he would slough off my fears with that gay, ironic way of his. I was only a boy and could hardly accuse him of anything. I was sure of nothing, anyway. And he was, after all a gentleman and a friend of mother's. He had been kind and helpful to her. Yet . . . I seemed to remember with a twinge that fierce look he had given me when he asked me to keep the secret of Fat Jack's map. I remember the slight chill that had touched me even then.

Valdez's house was silent. There was no light inside, though the sun had long ago set and night had descended. I rang the bell but no one came to the door. I tried the handle and the door opened.

Inside, I called several times, thinking that Valdez's servant may have been in the patio and failed to hear the ring of the bell.

I should have left then. But I went on through the entrance hall and into a room that looked like a study. I was looking for a scrap of paper and a pencil so I could write a note.

Against the left-hand wall of the room was a big roll-top desk. I tried it. It was unlocked. As I was rummaging around for pencil and paper my eye happened to fall on an open book lying to one side of the desk top. A book marker was aslant across the right-hand page.

I found the pencil and paper and began my note, asking Valdez to come to the shop that evening. I couldn't decide whether to mention the wine and had paused, pencil to my lips, when my eyes idly scanned the open book.

I started at the word *Belladonna* in boldface type. The book was a sort of pharmaceutical dictionary, very old

and dog-eared, written in English. Curiosity or fate—
something made me read more closely:

"Deadly nightshade or *atropa belladonna* is a tall,
bushy herb that grows to a height of four or five
feet having leaves of a dull green color with a black,
shining berry fruit. The entire plant is highly poisonous, the active constituent being atropine (C_{12}
$H_{23} NO_3$). Atropine may be easily extracted from
the roots or leaves by means of chloroform. The
medicinal dose is 1/200 grain to 1/50 grain. More
than this has an instant toxic effect, its severity depending upon the condition of the patient. Any
dose more than a grain is almost invariably lethal,
death resulting from respiratory and heart failure.
Emetics should be administered and heart stimu-
lant—large quantities of hot strong coffee proving effective. . . ."

The paragraph continued but I could read no more.
Deadly nightshade—I recognized the bush from this de-
scription as one which grew near the cemetery of Puerto
Del Sol. Stunned, I stood there like a statue, not knowing what to think, not daring to think the obvious thing.

I heard a noise, or thought I did. Frantically I stuffed
the note I had written into my pocket and replaced everything on the desk as I had found it. I tiptoed out the
back door; no one saw me. The alleyway was empty.

Valdez. Could he be a poisoner—that friendly, cul-
tured man? I remembered what Jap had said about gold:

it makes the best men crazy. I walked home slowly. The streets were dark. I found myself jumping at every sound, half afraid I would meet up with Valdez in his motor chair. I wouldn't have known how to hide my horror from his penetrating eyes.

7

I Find the Leather Hand

I decided to pass by the gin shop to tell the doctor to give Gordo some strong, black coffee. I wasn't going to implicate Valdez, not yet; it might all be a coincidence. But as I peeped through the gin shop door, I saw that my advice was no longer required. The doctor's emetic had done its work. Gordo was sitting up, shaking his head exactly as Jap had done. He seemed dazed; his cheeks were grimy and stained with tears.

"He'll come around now," the doctor told me. I decided to say nothing, and reassured, continued on my way home.

Facts and fancies crowded pell-mell through my head,

so many of them that when I looked up after fifteen minutes I was surprised to find myself already home, standing before the front door of the Kansas City. Only then did I observe that the house was completely dark. Mother must have gone straight to bed. But where was Paco?

I took out my key and felt around for the lock. The door swung inward at the touch of my fingers; it was hanging loose on its hinges. I struck a match and saw that the lock had been broken.

I ran inside, calling for mother and stumbled over a chair as I sought the light switch. In a moment the shop was flooded with light. Everything was orderly and tidy, everything in its niche except for the chair I had knocked over. The cashbox was intact. Why had the lock been forced if not for robbery? And where was my mother?

I ran down the hall which traversed the length of the house, turning on lights in every room. All was peaceful and serene, every piece of furniture in its appointed place, every vase and rug as it should be. At mother's bedroom door I knocked softly and listened. I called her. Hearing nothing, I thrust the door open. She was not there, but her bed had been slept in. The covers were tossed back. I called up and down the hall as loud as I could.

"Is that you, Ron?" Her voice came from the rear of the house, muffled and faint.

"Yes. Where are you?"

"In the kitchen."

I hurried to the kitchen at the far end of the hall. The door wouldn't open. It was bolted from inside. "Are you all right, mother?" I shouted.

"Yes, yes. Just a moment," came from behind the door.

Pressing my ear to the panel, I heard sounds as if someone were moving furniture. The bolt was shot back and I burst into the room. It was dark, but the light from the hallway revealed to me the pale face of my mother standing before me in her dressing gown. With a choked sob she ran up and flung her arms around me.

Soothing her, patting her hair, I let her cry, restraining my questions. I couldn't help craning my neck, searching the kitchen for some clue as to what had happened. As soon as my eyes became adjusted to the dim light, I saw that the door had not only been bolted, but barricaded as well. Mother had up-ended the kitchen table and braced it against the door. Two kitchen chairs were lying on their sides, and the lamp was flung to the floor.

In a short while mother's tears ceased. She blew her nose. "There now. I've quite recovered."

Leaving her side I stepped across to pick up the lamp.

"Watch out. You may get a shock," she said sharply.

I had the lamp in my hand. It had been severed from the connecting wire and was dead. "The light doesn't work," I said.

"Yes, I know." She stooped and picked up a long electric wire, frayed at the end. "There," she said. "Now you won't get hurt."

I saw with amazement that the kitchen table lamp—the only light in that inconvenient kitchen—had been torn away from its wire. It was this wire, still plugged into the wall socket, that mother held now, very gingerly, pointing the charged and naked end away from herself.

"What has happened? Who ripped the lamp from the wire?" I said. "Be careful, mother or you'll give yourself a jolt."

"*I* tore the lamp off the wire," she said.

"*You* did?"

"Yes. Someone broke into the shop. I was frightened and thought I'd better defend myself. I couldn't possibly use a knife or anything like that—it would make me sick to my stomach. So I thought that a smart electrical shock would scare anyone away without really hurting him."

It was the oddest weapon I had ever heard of. Just like a woman to get such an idea. I couldn't help laughing.

My laughter moved her to tears again. She was unstrung. The scene at the gin shop—and now the intruder—had proved too much for her.

I righted one of the chairs, searched in the tool drawer for pliers and a knife, and, as mother leaned back and told me what had occurred, I fixed the lamp.

She had retired as soon as she had arrived home. "I had a cup of broth and then went right to bed. I was feeling jumpy and sad, as you know." Paco had been in the patio stacking wood but had gone out soon after. She heard him lock the back door. Half an hour later or less, she was awakened by someone tinkering with the lock at the shop door.

Thinking I had forgotten my key, she got out of bed and started down the hall when she heard the lock forced and the front door swing open. She stood glued to the spot in the dark hall, listening. Then she saw a ray of light moving beneath the crack of the door which separated the shop from the rest of the house.

"Who's there?" she called out. The light was extinguished and all was silent.

Half paralyzed, she remained in the hall, leaning against the wall for support. The house was utterly still.

Then she heard the faintest of sounds—the stealthy, almost imperceptible click of a door handle being slowly turned. The door from the shop was opening inch by inch, not ten feet in front of her.

With a cry she ran back down the hall and into the kitchen, the only room in the house with a bolt, barricaded herself in and waited, armed with the charged wire.

"I've been here almost an hour," she said. "I heard nothing more until you came."

The lamp was repaired. I snapped it on. Troubled as I was about the inexplicable intruder, I was more troubled at the sight of my mother's face, the dark circles under her eyes and the nervous way she bit her lips. She was strained almost to the breaking point and must be forced to rest. But I couldn't leave her alone in the unlocked house and didn't know how I was going to get the doctor. We had no telephone.

I cursed Paco. Stupid as he was, he could have carried a message for me. Then I wondered: had he staged the whole scene himself? If so, there could have been only one thing he was after—the model of the sampan which he had overheard Jap and me talking about the night we discovered him outside my door. At Jap's suggestion, I had recently taken it from the shop and placed it in my room as an additional safeguard.

"Come on, mother," I said. "Let's get out of the kitchen. There's nothing more to be frightened of. The robber has gone, and taken nothing. You must have scared him off, for the shop is as neat as a pin."

Mother was anxious to check over the stock. I left her in the shop and went across the hall to my room. There on my bed was the sampan model, broken apart. I felt inside the hollow mast and found it empty. Neddie's map was gone.

I felt a surge of relief. Yes, I was lighthearted with relief. I understood now why Jap had been so anxious to unburden his secret to me. I, too, was glad to be free of it. I felt a spiteful elation in the knowledge that the map wouldn't do its new owner any good. No one but Jap, with his fantastic agility under water and his keen understanding of the sea, could ever find the red cave and figure out how to get inside it. But even if someone were able to make his way into the cave he would find what we had found—an immovable treasure.

Smiling, I returned to the shop. "Nothing in the house has been touched," I said, resolved not to worry mother by telling her about the sampan.

Mother was sitting on a stool. "It looks all right here, too," she said. "But I don't feel up to checking everything. I'm tired, Ron." Weariness was evident in the tonelessness of her voice. But she refused to go to bed. "I want to let my nerves settle a bit."

I decided to improvise a chain for the door so that I

could lock it with a padlock and then go for the doctor. I was searching for tools and a chain among the stock drawers when there came a faint tap-tap at the door. It was pushed gently inward and there in the darkness sat Valdez. He was smiling.

Involuntarily I quivered and shrank back. I couldn't meet his eyes. But my mother gave a glad little cry. "Oh, Mr. Valdez, how lucky that you came by."

"Good evening, good evening," he said, rolling his chair into the room. "I saw the shop lights blazing. You're open very late this evening, milady."

"Oh, Mr. Valdez, the most terrible thing. . . ." And mother began telling her story. I watched Valdez's face intently. If he were in any way implicated, he was a superb actor. Even I, who had seen with my own eyes the book on his desk, began to doubt my suspicions. I found myself ashamed of them.

There was something compelling about Valdez; he compelled belief. There are people like that—people whom one may detest and mistrust when they are absent, but whose presence instantly dispels all antagonisms. I have met several since—men whom I knew to be cheats and liars—yet when talking to them face to face I have found myself again and again relaxing all defenses, compelled to believe.

Two hours before, I had felt a loathing for Valdez, a loathing mixed with dread and fear. Now, I found myself warming to him, actually glad he had come. Already he had my mother smiling; soon she was gay and laughing. His big, weather-beaten face, bitten deep with lines of character, was attentive, graciously smiling. He was teasing my mother a little. When she told him about the electric wire, he burst into a laugh. "That's the most original weapon it's been my experience to encounter. My congratulations."

Mother blushed with pleasure. Soon she was telling him about Jap's attack and about Gordo. He seemed genuinely shocked. "And in this place they'll never find the guilty person," he said with mild indignation. "You know how the police are here. Their incompetence is monumental."

Suddenly mother said: "Come on back in the kitchen, Mr. Valdez. I'll make you a cup of tea and have one myself." She rose.

I spoke up. "Mother, I was wondering if Mr. Valdez would be kind enough to get the doctor for us. We haven't any sedatives in the house and you'll sleep better if you have one after all the excitement."

"I'd be delighted to be of service," said Valdez.

"You see, I hate to leave mother alone after what happened," I explained.

"Oh Ron," said mother, "I'm not alone when I'm with Mr. Valdez. He'll protect me. And to tell the truth, I'm rather enjoying myself. It's not often I'm able to play the heroine." She laughed. "You run along and find the doctor, Ron. Though I don't really need anything now, just a cup of tea."

I had no choice but to leave her with Valdez.

They went down the hall to the kitchen while I fastened the shop door with some bent wire. My hands were beginning to hurt again; the bandages made manual work difficult, and I had already broken the skin in a couple of places when fixing the kitchen lamp. Before going out I went into my room to take a closer look at the ship model. It had been ruthlessly broken and there was no possibility of putting it together, not even with glue. I hid the pieces at the bottom of my closet to make sure mother wouldn't find them. She didn't know, of course, about the map; but she would have been put-out to find the model broken after promising Jap to take care of it.

I peeped into the kitchen before leaving by the back door. There were mother and Valdez as thick as thieves and chattering away like two magpies. Valdez was wheeling himself here and there as mother directed: "Now, while I blow up the coals, you may as well make yourself useful. You'll find the cups and saucers in the cupboard there, and the sugar is in the red cannister."

"Aye, aye, mum," said Valdez, imitating Paco.

Holding cups, saucers and spoons in his single hand, he propelled the chair with his elbows and laid out the tablecloth as neatly as you please. One could hardly have witnessed a more domestic scene. And I had thought the man a poisoner! I felt like a fool—naïve, tricked by too much imagination.

I called a good-bye through the door and stepped across the patio into the alleyway, deciding that I would try to catch the doctor at Gordo's; with luck he might still be there. I knew a short cut through the crisscross of alleys which would get me to the gin shop in five minutes. The going was a bit uncertain; the people of Puerto Del

Sol weren't the tidiest in the world and had a way of dumping everything, from old rags to dead cats, into the alley. But I had a flashlight.

After a block I turned into a narrow back lane between two high garden walls, almost like a canyon. Hurrying at the turn, I veered aside to bypass a cluster of garbage cans and almost stepped on a man who was half crouched behind the cans. It was Paco.

"Hey!" I said, turning the flashlight on him. He made no move to get away, just stood there looking at me vacantly and blinking in the light.

"There you are, you ruffian," I said, catching hold of him by the shoulder. "What are you doing here? Where have you been?"

I must have spoken more roughly than I intended, for he literally shrank away from me. "I'm on my way home, sir," he said with trembling lips. "I heard footsteps and tried to hide. I didn't want to meet any robbers. I didn't guess it would be you, sir."

"Robbers! What do you know about robbers? Anyway, what have you got that a robber might want?"

"Nothing, sir. Nothing absolutely."

We two were alone in the steep and silent alley. I could see he was half frightened out of his wits at my sudden appearance. He was a coward by nature, a habitual cringer without the slightest streak of bluff or bravado in his make-up. I had never met a more craven person, and here I had him fairly cornered. It struck me that the circumstances were ideal for forcing a showdown, for getting out of him whatever he knew about the events of the last days. In that narrow alley there was no chance for escape; besides, I held fast to his coat sleeve. And there were no listeners to intimidate him into hedging. I felt that I could threaten and dominate him unmercifully here. By mere superior strength of will, I could force the truth out of him.

"Listen here, Paco," I whispered between clenched teeth, bending close and scowling, putting on a show of violent temper, "I don't like the way you're acting. I'm going to fire you. Now. In ten minutes. Unless you talk straight. Why are you hiding out here?"

"I just told you, sir. I was walking home when . . ."

"Yes, I know. Afraid of robbers. All right, let's see what's in your pockets that a robber would want. Come on."

To my surprise he showed no hesitancy in complying and began at once to empty his pockets. He only had three, his trouser pockets. He was not wearing a coat, just a T shirt, an old one of mine that mother had given him. He placed the contents of his pockets one by one on the lid of the nearest garbage can, where my flashlight played over them; then he dutifully turned the pockets inside out, dropping a shower of dust and grime from the greasy linings.

I had expected to see the map of the *Mary F.*—Neddie's half—among Paco's treasures. But I was sadly mistaken. Indeed, I felt moved to compassion at the shoddiness of the little treasures he hoarded—rusted screws, a wad of lead foil, a small pocket knife that was tied to its handle by a twist of wire, a coil of tarred string, a fish-hook, a folder of matches and so on—the contents of a boy's pockets, not very different from the gewgaws I had treasured myself not more than five years ago.

The sight of this sorry heap on the garbage-can lid—and Paco's hangdog hope that I would find nothing in it to take issue with—made me feel petty and not a little ridiculous.

"Put them back," I said roughly, feeling it a duty to hide my sympathy. "No robber would want any of that stuff." Then, thinking I might have let him off too easily, I added: "Just a minute. Take off your shoes." The map might be there, I thought. And when he kicked off his shoes and held them out for my inspection I saw paper inside.

Pointing, I said: "What's that?"

He turned the shoes over and I saw that several folded bits of newspaper had been inserted to cover two gaping holes in the soles. The sight of those pitiful shoes completed my interrogation. I wanted no more of it.

"It's all right," I said gently.

As he jammed his feet back into the shoes and refilled his pockets I felt, in spite of myself, a sense of pity. I knew he was an orphan, but I had never before sensed what it must mean to be penniless, homeless, and friendless in Puerto Del Sol—and Paco had been all these while still a child. He must have had to cringe all his life, ever since he could remember. Cringing and fawning must have been his only means of survival, a means learned early and in a bitter school, the streets.

I could no longer play the bullying master with him. I

felt humble. Pity always makes me feel humble and un-
worthy of my own luck.

He straightened up and I asked him as simply as I
could, without that coldness and haughtiness I had been
using, "You spoke of robbers. What made you think of
that?"

He shifted his eyes and hung his head, alert again to
danger.

"Did you know that the shop had been broken into?"

He said nothing.

"You *did* know," I guessed. "You should not have left
the señora alone." I spoke without rancor, as if chiding a
child.

"I . . . I went to get the police," he said, brightening
suddenly and looking bashfully at me. It was the most
pathetic of lies. Paco, as I knew, was more afraid of the
police than he could ever be of a thief. The police had
ragged him and beaten him for sport when he was a street
boy grubbing in garbage cans and sleeping under porch
steps.

But by pretending to believe this lie and thus allowing
him to save face, I got the story out of him. It was a short
one and not very noble. He had been stacking wood in
the patio when darkness obliged him to leave off. He had
entered the kitchen to wash up, not yet having turned on
the light, when he heard someone prowling around the
house, trying the windows. That was all. He had simply
left the house as quietly as he could—crept away, and had
been hiding in the alley ever since.

Of course, he didn't tell me this ending exactly as I've

told it here. He had gone for the police; he kept to that part, insisted on it to save his self-respect. I didn't ask why he had failed to find the police. The town headquarters with a complement of four men was not fifteen minutes away and there was always a man on night duty. Such a question would have been too heartless.

"All right, Paco," I said. "You can go home now. The thief broke the lock, but he's gone. He took nothing. Perhaps you can help the señora by fixing up a chain for the front door." Smiling and thanking me profusely (a matter of habit, for he had nothing to thank me for that he knew of, unless he guessed at my pretended belief in his fib about the police) he shuffled off toward home. I went on to get the doctor.

I bumped into the doctor coming out of the gin shop and took him directly home with me. He looked grave at the sight of mother's flushed face and overexcited manner. It was plain that she was overwrought by the events of the day, and in a state of excitement that was not normal. Her eyes were afire. She protested that she was feeling wonderful, better than usual, but the doctor gently suggested that she retire and get some sleep.

I left him with mother in the kitchen preparing a sedative powder. He was a gentle and kindly person, Dr. Sanchez—a man in his sixties who had practiced in our port for thirty-five years. In his youth he had been ruined by a terrible incident from which he had never recovered. On coming to Puerto Del Sol from his studies abroad, in the first flush of enthusiasm he had persuaded the town authorities to let him vaccinate all school children against smallpox, the cost to be borne by himself.

Twenty children died. The serum had been incompetently manufactured. Dr. Sanchez was exonerated of blame and the pharmaceutical firm, a fly-by-night outfit, was shown to have been at fault. But morally speaking the doctor held himself to account. He never overcame the effects of this disaster on his spirit; it marked him throughout his life. He was the soul of gentleness and compassion, but in his practice he was inclined to trust to nature rather than to medicine. He seemed never to advise anything but sedatives and hope.

The doctor's melancholy, stooped figure had attracted mother from the first, and when she heard his story she would have no other doctor. His manner was most effective with her, just what she needed—calming and sobering. I heard him speaking to her, as I left the kitchen, in his soothing, unhurried voice—already quieting the excitement which was burning her energies to ill effect.

I went down the passage with Valdez to let him out the front door. I was pushing his chair, talking and gossiping with him. I had forgotten all my fear of him. I was speaking away as naturally as one speaks to any long-time acquaintance.

Mother had been telling him about our life back home in Newton, I guessed, for he was full of questions. I found myself answering eagerly, praising as I always did those limitless prairies of my childhood. I had scarcely noticed them when I lived in Kansas, but now I often thought of them with an ache of nostalgia. I described the vista south toward Wichita—the flat land, mile upon mile of it, rippling with ripe grain; with here and there a trickling line of pale cottonwoods to mark the banks of a creek; the steep-pitched red barns, the round silos, and the fragrance of the earth. The smell of the prairie on a summer night—I can never describe it, so dry, so sweet, so haunting it is.

"Young man," said Valdez, smiling, "you sound ready to take the first boat back."

"Oh, I'll go back," I said. "I'll go back someday. This place can never be home to me."

There was a silence. I wondered if I hadn't talked too much.

At last Valdez said: "I, too, shall go back to my land, to the dripping jungles, brilliant and cruel. I love them as much as you love your far-flung prairies." There was a faraway look in his eyes. Then he laughed lightly—bitterly it seemed to me. I saw his jaw set and the muscles of his cheek tighten. "Soon, too. I have business to settle back there."

I opened the door and wheeled him out onto the sidewalk.

"Until tomorrow. I'll drop by to see how your mother is feeling." Valdez held out his hand and gripped mine in a friendly, almost affectionate way.

The air had grown chill in the last hour; a sea wind was whirling down the street. Valdez shivered.

I said: "Let me run inside and get a scarf for you."

"Don't bother. I have one. In the left saddlebag there,

son, if you'd be kind enough to reach for it. And a cap,
too, for my ears."

I felt in the saddlebag. My hand touched something
unexpected, something hard. It was large, filling most of
the bag. I felt around its firm edges but found no scarf.
Valdez was talking on. I was not listening. A horrible
suspicion had taken hold of me.

I withdrew the curious thing I had touched and stood
looking at it, frozen; my limbs turned to water. I was
holding a stuffed leather forearm with a leather hand
dangling from it. Fortunately I was behind Valdez's
chair. He could not see my face.

"Here. Here's the scarf," he said gaily. "I had it here
in my pocket all the time." He half turned to see me
hastily replacing the fearful leather contraption.

Abruptly he ceased speaking and glanced shrewdly and
sharply at me.

I could not look at him. There was a short silence; like
a dead hand it seemed to separate us.

Then he recovered himself with a laugh: "I see you've
discovered my ugly secret—my spare hand. Sometimes,
you know, I find myself alone with no one to help me—to
open doors and drawers and take off my clothes. I can
manage by myself with that thing."

My throat was as dry as dust. I was literally unable to
speak.

Valdez took the thing from me and adroitly buckled it
onto the amputated stump of his left arm. It snapped
into place below the elbow by means of some clever metal
clamps and a leather strap. His stump disappeared neatly

into the padded hollow and he now looked as if he had a whole arm, sheathed in leather up to the elbow. The hand was attached to the forearm with soft, pliant leather and could be flicked up and down ingeniously, looking almost like a real hand that is limp.

"There you are," said Valdez holding it up for my inspection. I was utterly speechless, my eyes starting out of my head. I couldn't believe that he failed to see my agitation.

I stayed behind the chair under the pretext of pushing him along the sidewalk, as he demonstrated his agility with the leather hand. "It's filled with lead. A handy weapon," he said cheerfully. Was I mistaken, or was there a veiled implication in his words?

He unbuckled the arm and threw it casually back into the saddlebag. "I don't like to wear it in public," he said. "It's an ugly thing—hideous but effective." Then cheerfully he started the motor of his chair and was soon chugging off down the street, waving pleasantly.

I didn't sleep that night in spite of the fact that I was half dead with fatigue. I could hardly believe that only that morning I had set off with Jap on our jolly expedition; so much had happened since to turn the day into a nightmare. All my horror and fear of Valdez engulfed me again until I seemed to see that leather arm striking at me from the dark above my bed. Yet he was a cripple, unable to rise unaided from his chair. Or was his paralysis a sham—as much a sham as were his graciousness and kindness?

Toward morning I heard my mother begin to cough;

it seemed to me that she would never stop. I lay there for hours, it seemed, listening to that dry nervous cough. I have never felt more despondent in my life than I did that morning as the dreary dawn came through my shutters.

Jap and I Get the Treasure

Though mother insisted on getting up as usual and going through her morning routine—making the beds, preparing breakfast, and opening the shop—I could see she was exerting an effort. When she thought no one was looking she would stop, lean against a chair, and brush her forehead with the back of her hand. I heard that dry short cough again; it penetrated me like a knife. The doctor in Newton had told me to watch out for that cough. Mother said it came from a "tickle" in her throat and was nothing. But the doctor had warned me that such a cough, though purely nervous in origin, was a dan-

116

ger sign because it indicated that her spirit was sagging
and her defenses, on the point of giving up.

Mother was young and vital, but like a plant she
needed the sun to flourish. Her sun was orderliness, habit,
and most of all a trust in the decency and humaneness of
her fellows. This trust had been shattered by the events of
the day before . . . the poisoned wine followed by the
prowler. These denied the seemliness of existence, outraged it, and left her in a state of uneasiness that told on
her health. I recognized the signs—the same bewildered
withdrawal I had witnessed after my father's unexpected
death.

Dr. Sanchez assured me that there was no sign of active
tuberculosis. How did he know, I wondered? He had
taken no X ray.

The doctor had come to the shop at nine, before his
daily rounds. I sat in whispered consultation with him in
the living room after he had talked to mother and ex-
amined her. She was out of earshot in the shop.

"I'm sure your fears are unfounded, my boy, though
natural," he said. "Your mother is a spirited woman."

"But if her spirit has been broken?"

He shrugged lightly and sighed. "Nature heals all
wounds, if God wills."

This answer was far from satisfying to me. I possessed
the natural hotheadedness of youth; I vehemently re-
jected such fatalism. I could not sit back and do nothing.

"Dr. Sanchez," I said, "forgive me, but you must do
your utmost."

"Yes, yes," he said in his soothing voice.

I was ready to shake him. "Aren't you going to do *any-thing?* Is there nothing?"

"Patience, my dear boy. Patience and time. It's wiser to wait. Your mother's will to live will conquer."

I suppose he was right, but I saw red. With difficulty I controlled myself, and when he was gone I threw his prescription on the table in disgust. Sedatives, fortifiers—mere palliatives!

Anxiety made it impossible for me to remain idle. I decided to have a talk with Jap. He knew as yet nothing of our prowler and the broken sampan, nor of Gordo's attack nor of the book I had seen on Valdez's desk. Besides, an idea had just occurred to me concerning my mother. I ran off to Jap's as fast as I could go.

He was in his patio weaving a fish net for a friend, sitting on the tiles and twisting the wooden bobbin in and out like a shuttlecock. He held the strings taut with his big toe like a monkey on a stick. He seemed completely recovered from the sickness of yesterday and grinned as I burst into the patio.

"Jap," I began at once, "can't we pick out the gold with a pickaxe? Can't we pry it out, melt it out—something? Just a little? Just enough to get my mother out of here?"

Though I had said all this in a jumble of breathlessness, Jap knew it was serious and considered his answer carefully. He ran his hand through his hair and then said one word: "Yes."

Still thoughtful, watching my face, he repeated: "Yes.

Jap think with crowbar and hammer we get some. Gold soft metal."

"Will you help me do it?"

"Sure. I help."

"When can we go? Do you feel all right?"

"Jap okay. How you hands?"

My hands were still sore, but I said: "They don't matter. The water will sting, but what of that? Jap, my mother's likely to be very sick unless I get her away—quick. We haven't enough money from the shop. I don't want the treasure, though. All I want is enough to pay a passage to the nearest big city, Madrid, I guess . . . a specialist's fee . . . and then . . . to do whatever he tells us. But all that will cost more than we have, much more. I'm scared. The doctor here doesn't have an X-ray machine, and poor man, he's afraid to do anything."

Jap said: "Want to go now?"

"Yes."

"Good. We go."

"Listen, Jap," I said as he, still seated, began winding up his fish-net twine, "listen, there are some things you ought to know. I've found someone who has a leather hand."

Jap waited, looking at my face intently.

"It's Valdez."

He did not seem surprised; he nodded and then returned to his work. "How did you find out?" he asked quietly.

I told him. I also told him about Gordo's attack and

about finding the book on Valdez's desk with the marked passage on deadly nightshade.

"Mother gave the lunch basket to him," I said. "He could have tampered with the wine thermos."

Jap said nothing, so I went on. I told him about the housebreaker and about the map being gone. When I had finished speaking he threw aside his bobbin and half-woven net and stood up. He walked across the patio once and then stood in front of me.

"Ron. You remember long time back Jap say: gold cost blood? Look, Ron, Jap save money. I got three, four hundred dollar saved up. I give you. You leave gold alone. Forget gold."

I was touched. But I could not take his life savings. "Thank you, Jap," I said. My voice was unsteady. I felt a surge of almost uncontrollable affection for this loyal and upright friend. "No, I can't take your money. Besides, I'm not afraid. I only want enough gold to help my mother. I'm not going to shed blood for it."

He sighed. "I give all I have with glad heart."

"No, Jap . . . no."

"All right. But, pardon me, you fool not be afraid. I scared, plenty scared. Listen: Valdez, he sure mixed up here some way. Everything point Valdez. Jap poisoned. Then we find Valdez touch jug, Valdez study how make poison. What else? Valdez big man, have leather hand. Jap beaten by big man with leather hand."

"But, Jap, he's a helpless cripple. You said the big man was walking around in your room."

"How you know he cripple? He say so. Lots peoples tell lies. And now what happen? Sampan stolen, map gone. Valdez do that, too, I think. He mad for gold. You know what? Jap think Valdez know all about gold long time. He always hire men to dig, dig in Frenchmen's Woods while he watch like cat. But can't find."

Jap was right; everything pointed to Valdez. And Valdez himself had told me that his purpose in coming to Puerto Del Sol had been Fat Jack's map. Jap knew nothing of this, but his guess was cheek by jowl with the truth.

Jap went on: "I think Valdez got map now. Yellow cross show pretty close, pretty damn close to cave. He going tear up whole coast now. He hire people dynamite, I bet. That man a devil. You see how his eye shine at night like cat's?"

I made an attempt to laugh.

"No. Don't laugh. Listen, I tell more. Every day since I show that gold money you mama—remember?—he follow me around. I see him everywhere. He always near Jap. Like he keep watch. He think I got more gold money."

"Maybe you're right, Jap. Sometimes I think the way you do, but when I see him he seems so friendly that I don't know what to think. Anyway, if we go out now, we'll get out some gold—the little we want—and there won't be anything Valdez can do, or anyone, *whoever*, it is."

Jap shook his head. "What you mean? That just what he want. We get gold. Then he take." He drew his finger across his throat. "That man a devil."

We were in the bright morning sunlight of the patio, but I shivered. "I've *got* to get the money," I said firmly.

"Okay. Better we go night time. No one see."

The idea of delay dismayed me, though I realized Jap was right. A man who would poison was capable of anything. It was wiser to be cautious. I still was not convinced that Valdez was our enemy; I didn't want to be convinced, that was it. I was drawn to the man. But events had proved that someone was after the gold and after Jap, and caution was the watchword.

We agreed to meet at the dock at 8:45, an hour after sunset, near the unlighted north embankment where we could embark unnoticed. Jap would moor the boat there during the day. "I go out catch fish to sell," he explained. "No one guess. Then I put boat in hide place—you know, where trees touch water." He said he would load the equipment beforehand, also a crowbar and hammer and two bags for carrying out the gold, and lots of twine. Fishermen always carry twine for a dozen different uses. "We got swim twenty yards under water. Can't have big sack. Too much weight. I got some little bags.

"One more thing," he said as I was leaving. "That man, maybe he no got good legs. But he buy legs easy, buy people run for him. You know what? I see him one day give money to you fellow, that ugly fellow work for you mama. Paco."

"You saw Valdez give money to Paco!" I stopped short in the doorway.

"Yes."

"But why?"

"Maybe Paco be that Mr. Valdez's legs. Run for him. Spy for him."

"But why? Why? Valdez doesn't act like a man who's thirsty for money. He seems to be comfortably off. He lives modestly. Why?" I shook my head, confused. I couldn't believe Valdez was a poisoner and a liar, because . . . because I didn't want to believe it. I felt that there must be some other explanation.

Jap spread out his hands and shrugged. "He got reasons he don't tell nobody. Every man got secrets he don't tell."

I left then. Jap's last words were a warning: "Don't tell nobody we go tonight. Or we run into trouble, I bet. Big trouble."

Unfortunately I was not able to keep this wise injunction. I had to tell my mother. She was so distressed at seeing me prepare to leave after dark that I couldn't bring myself to slough off her anxiety with a trivial lie. It would have hurt her to think I was running out to gad about when she wasn't well.

"Ron, you're not going swimming at this hour?" She had seen the roll of my bathing trunks and towel.

I faced her and placed my hands on her shoulders. "Mother, I'm going to tell you something and you're going to listen and obey me, as you promised to do. I am going out in Jap's boat. I shall be away about three hours. And tomorrow we start packing. . . ."

"Packing? Where are we going?"

"Wherever you want to go, mother. After what's happened I don't imagine you want to stay on here. Tell me, where do you want to go? We'll go anywhere you say."

She lifted her hand to her mouth to stifle a little cry—a cry of surprise and joy. Tears filled her eyes. She spoke softly. "Oh Ron, I know it's wrong of me after we've come all the way out here, but . . . I long for . . . for home." She shook her head lightly and gave a little laugh. "But that's a silly dream. How could we ever afford it?"

"You mustn't ask questions," I said. "Please forgive me this secrecy, but it's better. The whole story is too long to tell you now."

In a low voice she said: "You've found the British gold."

I put my finger to her lips and said nothing.

"But our house in Newton is sold, Ron. We've no place to go back to."

"Shhh. We'll talk all that over tomorrow. Here's something to think about meantime: I've heard that the old Roundy place is for sale, up at the northeast quarter section by the Solomon River. The doctor wrote me."

"The old Roundy place . . ." Her voice was dream-like. "Home. It's funny. What I miss most of all are the seasons. There's no spring here, no autumn . . . the maple leaves all red and the sumac. And the smells of spring when the snow melts, that tenderness in the air of April . . ." She was crying softly.

"I'll be back soon," I said, kissing the top of her head.

Dr. Sanchez's wife had come to spend the evening with mother. I left the two of them together in the kitchen. Mrs. Sanchez was a duplicate of her husband, a sad, soft, ineffectual creature—not the cheeriest companion for a woman who needed her spirits lifted. But she was a good soul and, besides, thoughts of home, I knew, would be mother's real companions that evening.

I left the house exactly at eight-thirty as the moon was rising.

The sea was smooth that night and the sky cloudless. The surface of the water was radiant with moon rays. Jap and I rowed north along the shore until we were well away from town. Only then did we hoist the sail and head directly across the bay.

I felt certain we had made our departure unobserved, but Jap shook his head doubtfully. "Lots people see," he said. "Maybe they good peoples." It was true that in a town as small as Puerto Del Sol a man couldn't take a walk to the barber's without its being known. Everyone knew everyone else, and idleness made every man curious about his neighbor. Jap was right no doubt; many people —loafers, shopkeepers, fishermen—had probably remarked us separately heading toward the clump of tamarisks that hid the boat. But if luck were with us they were disinterested people who didn't care a whit about our errand that night.

I kept looking backward as our little boat cut a swath across the headwaters of the bay, anxious to see if a boat were following. Such a search was useless. It was the squid season, and a dozen boats at least could be seen dotting the water, each with its alcohol lantern aglow. None appeared to be keeping to the same course as ourselves, so I ceased worrying and put my trust in luck and speed. I was too excited to worry; this expedition meant much to me and I bent my energies towards the goal.

We made excellent time. Within twenty minutes we had anchored off the rocks above the red cave. We descended into the water at once, Jap going ahead with the light and I swimming close at his heels. This time the swim through the undersea passage seemed easy. I made it with breath to spare, though I was weighted with the tools and had a large gunny sack wrapped around my waist like a cummerbund.

It was Jap's idea to bring along the sack. For storage, he said. Optimistically thinking we might loosen more coins than we could carry out in our two small bags, he had decided it would be foolish to leave loose coins lying in the hollow. They might be washed away. We could put them in the gunny sack and leave it high and dry above the water line, securing it on a shelf of rock. "Safe like a bank," he had said. "We come back when we want more, eh? Take out—like rich man."

Jap had also brought along a length of cord, some candles, and matches which he had placed in an empty mayonnaise jar corked and sealed watertight. The candles were to provide light while we worked; he didn't want to risk keeping his lamp alight for fear the battery would give out. We needed the lamp to get out. No one, not even, Jap, could find the exit passage without an undersea light.

As I swam full speed along the passage I remembered only too well how glad I had been to get out of that weird cave before, with its reddish glow and flickering shapes.

This time I determined to keep my attention fastened on
the business at hand and in the long run I succeeded. But
for a moment when the candles were lighted I felt the
spell closing in on me. The candles, four of them, made
a far less steady light than Jap's lamp. An air vent from
one of the fissures swept over the candle flames, making
them jump and gutter. The whole cave seemed to be
dancing with ghosts and shadows amid the never-ceasing
thunder of the rushing water.

The niche in which the gold lay was part of a narrow
ledge; there was little room to work in, little to stand on.
Both of us, one on either side of the hollow, were in danger of losing our footing every moment. There was no
elbow room, either, for manipulating the tools. I gashed
my elbow the first time I made a stroke with the hammer,
and I was in terror that something—my metal wedge, the
hammer, one of the bags—would slip out of my grip and
sink beneath the water where, most likely, an hour would
be lost trying to find it again among the tufts of algae. On
top of everything else, we were both shivering with the
cold. The cave—never touched by the sun—was as dank
and clammy as the inside of an ice chest; it seemed colder
than on our last visit.

Wet, cold, and discouraged we started—I with the
hammer and wedge, Jap with the crowbar. My elbow was
bleeding profusely and my eyes were smarting from the
smoke of the candles. With the first stroke of the hammer, the raw blisters on my hands had burst. I remember
looking down at that dully-glowing pile of guineas with
anger and resentment.

Strangely enough, after this unpropitious beginning, the gold proved easy to pick out. Coin after coin snapped loose, like buttons popping off a fat man's jacket. The barnacles and shells that held the gold fast, on close examination, proved to be not so tough as expected. The lime and calcium deposits were stuck only to the edges of the coins, not the flat sides. By placing my wedge aslant at the edge of a coin and giving it a smart crack with the hammer, I found it an easy task to break the small, enclosing circle of sea cement all at a blow. The coin flipped an inch or two upward and was put in the gunny sack. Soon coins began to clink against one another within the sack.

The wedge being smaller proved more effective than the crowbar. After a while I got a certain knack. I became so proficient at judging the exact spot against which to give the quick, forceful tap that I was snapping up coins all around, never wasting two blows on a single coin. Not a few plopped into the water, lost forever. But there were so many more that I didn't spare a sigh for them. Jap gave up working with the clumsy crowbar and had enough to do raking in the guineas as I pried them loose.

I don't know how long we worked. It seemed a short time to me. A kind of nervous gaiety came over me; I was enjoying myself, proud of my dexterity at this strange type of gold digging. I had no idea how many coins I had pried loose. The hollow proved deep. The work got harder as I delved into the third and fourth layers. The angle of the wedge had to be kept almost parallel to the flat of the coins, and the space became very restricted. I had no room in which to swing the hammer. But I worked on—one more, one more—twisting myself into precarious positions and managing to keep my balance as if I were a tightrope performer.

Suddenly Jap said: "Say, boy. How much gold you want?"

I stopped. Poor Jap was blue with the cold. I felt heated, even feverish. I noticed that the candles were half burned away and smoking terribly.

"How much do we have?" I asked.

"Don't know. Plenty."

"Let's count them, Jap."

"You crazy? Let's go."

"Just a little while more," I said and started to work again. I began to count: "One, two, three . . . fifteen, sixteen, seventeen . . ."

I had picked out thirty more coins when Jap said: "Boy, you got gold fever."

I grinned. "Maybe I do. I feel I could go on and on. There must be thousands here. Look, we've hardly shaved off the top layers."

"We go now," said Jap, "or we never get out. The light, she going fast."

Reluctantly I tucked my tools in my belt. Making several trips along the rock shelf, we carried our paraphernalia and the gunny sack of gold to a flat space where we sat down. I was burning to count the gold. The gunny sack seemed heavy to me. I reached inside and felt the crusty, rough coins. Valdez had said that each one might be worth five or six dollars.

"We can't carry all that," said Jap.

I was disappointed. I hated to leave a single coin behind. But there was no way to take them out except in manageable quantities. We half-filled the two small bags —about twelve pounds in each. Any more weight might have hindered our passage out through the underwater tunnel. We hoisted the gunny sack, still bulging, high up on a dry ledge. Then, each with a small sack tied to his waist, we prepared to slip into the water. Jap blew out the candles, hung his lantern around his neck, and holding the tools in our hands we left the red cave for the last time. Neither of us ever entered it again.

The gold weighed me down more than I expected. That twenty-yard swim through the passage seemed long, longer than the minute and a half for which I could hold my breath. Once out, I kicked myself to the surface like a rocket, my lungs bursting. For a moment there, bobbing beneath the white radiance of the moon, gulping in the pure salt air, I was happier than I had ever been. I felt the hard, cold sack slapping against my thighs. And though I was treading water vigorously to keep it from dragging me under, I felt it was a precious weight.

Jap was swimming towards me. "Boat gone," he said quietly.

"The boat gone!" I could only repeat the words idiotically, all the while turning this way and that to scan the water. It's surface was as smooth as a platter. The little boat had disappeared; we were alone in the sea, two miles from home.

"Anchor rope cut," Jap said.

We couldn't talk there in the water. It was all we could do to keep our heads above it, dragged down as we were with twelve pounds of dead weight at our waists. Without another word we made for shore. Jap's lantern was still alight, but he snapped it off the moment we had climbed on the rocks. "We need light get home," he said.

Huddled together on the rocks, chilled to the bone, we held a whispered conference. Luckily Jap and I understood each other without many words; we could almost guess each other's thoughts. The conference was a quick one. I asked only one unnecessary question: "Are you sure the rope was cut?"

"What you think? You think Jap don't know tie knots? You think Jap use rotten rope? No sir. Somebody cut rope. And maybe he right here now, hide in trees behind us. Cut our throats, too."

That silenced me. I cast a glance over my shoulder at the dark trees of Frenchmen's Woods which loomed thick and black all along the shore to our right.

Jap asked: "Can you swim back?"

I longed to say I could; but I wasn't sure, cold as I was and with my hands raw and bleeding again. "I don't know," I said. "It's two miles and . . . well, I have doubts."

"Good boy. You honest boy, Ron. We walk home."

It wasn't going to be a picnic walking, either—even if we didn't encounter anyone bent on stopping our mouths and taking the gold. The nearest path was a mile inland;

the shortest way would be to keep to the coast, but the going was rocky, sharp lava rocks. And we were barefoot.

We decided to keep to the coast and to use the lantern sparingly to help us find the best footing.

"Now we get rid of gold," said Jap. I didn't question why. I knew well enough that those two sacks would exhaust us, would impede our progress. Also the very possession of them—in case we were ambushed by the person who had cut loose our boat—was a sure death sentence. We were armed, if you could call it that, with nothing more than a crowbar and a hammer. We hadn't even our spears. Everything . . . our clothes, Jap's knife, our watches, even the copy I had made of Neddie's map—all were lost in the boat. We never saw it again.

"You wait here," said Jap. "I find anchor." He untied his bag from his belt and threw it down beside me. Then lighting the lantern and pulling down his mask he swam out. I passed some bleak moments sitting there shivering in the moonlight, flanked by the two bags of coins. They were icy cold to the touch. But Jap was back in minutes. He had found the anchor on the bottom with its rope trailing along the sand beside it.

We emptied my bag of gold into his; it was now almost full. Then we tied the top securely and, carrying the sack between us, managed to swim out and tie it to the anchor. It was safe for a day or two, nestled on the bottom next to the anchor which would keep it from being rolled away by the current. To mark the spot Jap tied his cork-handled knife to the anchor with a ten-yard length of twine. It bobbled a few inches beneath the surface—a marker for him and for me, who would know what to look for and where, but unnoticeable to anyone else because it didn't break the surface.

In the empty bag that now remained we placed our tools, rope, goggles, and breathers. I slung it over my shoulder. Jap carried the lantern and led the way as we set out for home.

It was two in the morning when at last I crept into the Kansas City more dead than alive. Every bone of my body ached and every muscle. My feet were scarred and filthy and I thought I would never be warm again. On the sidewalk in front Jap whispered good-bye and took the bag from my shoulder. (We had taken turns carrying it.) "Good boy, Ron," he said, squeezing my hand in farewell. I was too tired to answer. I nodded. That was all. I've always regretted that I hadn't the energy to say something to that little man, the best friend I ever had. Little did I know that this ill-fated night was to be the last expedition we ever went on.

The hall light was on. I listened at my mother's door and heard her even breathing. She was asleep. In the kitchen I found a note from in which she said she had gone to bed at ten. She hadn't waited for me; I blessed her for that. She had been spared the anxiety of waiting until early morning.

The fire was out in the kitchen. Tired as I was I felt I couldn't get to sleep until I got warm, so I called softly for Paco. He slept on a cot in the room next to the woodshed. There was no answer, so I tiptoed out. I wanted him to make some tea for me and prepare a hot-water bottle—something so I could get warm.

With dull surprise I saw that he was not in his room. His bed had not been slept in. But I was too tired to think, to guess what this might mean. I dragged myself to my room and fell into bed, dirty and bloodstained as I was. I fell asleep as if I'd been struck with a mallet, my brain too dulled to contain a single thought.

9

I Am Left Alone

𝕹 *I was dreaming. It seemed that I was lost in a* vast ocean swimming against a stiff current. Then something grabbed me and began shaking me. I woke to find my mother shaking my shoulder.

"Ron! Ron! Something's happened. There's a terrible screaming down at the quay. Everyone is running down there."

I was instantly wide-awake. I pulled on my clothes and ran into the street and hurried along with a group of others—all heading for the quay. A dull roar, as of many voices, filled the air. Occasionally a woman's shriek rose above the other sounds, and oftener the bloodcurdling screams and yelps of someone in pain. Two shots rang out.

Nobody in the hurrying group knew what was happening. All were hastening, as I was, to find out. Their faces were stern and anxious; such a hullabaloo in the early dawn could only mean tragedy in our quiet town.

Running abreast with two men, I turned the last corner and emerged onto the wide cement quay. A crowd of some fifty persons was milling there, clustered around something near the edge of the embankment. There was another shot. People began shouting incoherently. I managed to hear a few isolated cries which told me nothing.

"Shoot him, Juan, shoot him!" a man was shouting over and over again.

"Steady your hand, man. Don't miss again," cried another.

I elbowed my way through the seething crowd and suddenly burst upon a sight the like of which I never wish to see again. Backed up against the edge of the quay, his teeth bared, his eyes glazed, stood Lobo, Jap's dog, holding the entire crowd at bay. Foam was slavering from his lips.

But the ghastly, unbelievable thing was—the dog's coat was aflame. Part of his fur was actually on fire, especially the long, thick hanks on top of his shoulders.

Two men were trying to push him backward into the water to put out the flames. But the dog held his ground. He was crazed with fear. I rushed forward.

For a split second Lobo didn't recognize me and I thought he was going to sink his fangs into my outstretched hand. But then suddenly he gave a shrill whine and, casting me a look of helpless appeal, bounded over to throw himself against me. I didn't know what to do.

"Shoot him! Put the poor creature out of his misery!" cried an overwrought woman.

"No! No!" I said, shielding Lobo with my body. I tried to think what to do and looked wildly to right and left for a bucket, a can, anything with which to dip up sea water and put out the flames. "A bucket! Get me a bucket!" I called.

There was a murmur of questions; then someone ran off. All the time Lobo's glazed eyes begged me to help him; a few seconds more and he would be completely on fire. I decided not to wait for the bucket. "Give me a coat, someone," I shouted, and a man handed me his jacket. But the moment I raised my arms to throw it over Lobo to smother the flames the dog cringed back and snarled. He thought I was going to harm him. Fear made him distrust even me.

I had no choice then. I threw the jacket aside and lunged forward, grasping the dog in a tight hug. He slashed my shoulder with his teeth. But I didn't feel them, for with all my strength I lifted the seventy-pound dog, strode two steps forward and leaped into the water, the dog in my arms.

That was all. In a hiss of steam we went under, Lobo's muscular body twisting violently in my grasp as we sank deep. But the flames were out. The dog struggled to the surface and swam to the quay as a dozen willing hands pulled him ashore. People were shouting my name:

"Bravo the American boy! Bravo for Ronaldo!"

Trembling now that it was over, I let myself be helped up also. Someone handed me a towel—not much use, as I was fully clothed. But I thanked the man and wiped my face with it. My shoulder wound was nothing, just a rip in the skin, and the sea water had cleansed it. I forgot about it.

I was anxious to examine Lobo. How badly had he been hurt? He lay shivering and panting on the cement, a most pitiable sight. Part of his fur was charred. But his muzzle, his eyes and ears were unhurt. He was a thick-furred dog and this had saved his skin from any serious damage. I stepped over to pat his wet, smoke-streaked head. He wagged his hairless tail. He would live.

"What happened?" I asked one of the men. "How did the poor animal catch its coat on fire?"

The man spit. "This wasn't an accident, señor. Didn't you smell the kerosene? The dog was soaked in it. Some beast of a man set the dog on fire." He looked away.

No one knew who had done it. The dog had come yelping onto the quay already blazing. Two fishermen had seen him first and tried to throw sea water on him with their hats. But the animal, half-crazed, had evaded their efforts, running in circles and fanning the flames that were eating his fur.

"Poor Jap," I thought, and I looked around for him, but he wasn't in the crowd. His absence struck me all at once as ominous. Lobo was never away from Jap's side except when Jap was fishing. What had he been doing away from home so early when Jap was still asleep in bed?

I was suddenly filled with dread. Where was Jap? Hastily instructing one of the men to take the dog to the veterinarian, where he would have to be kept in the sick kennel for several days while his burns were treated, I ran off to Jap's house as fast as I could go, wet clothes and all. At the edge of the plaza I bumped straight into Paco. He was leaning against a wall, mouth open, eyes glassy. I guessed that he had just witnessed the scene on the quay, but I didn't have time to ask him what was wrong.

"Paco!" I shook his shoulder. He blinked. "Wake up, man!"

"Yes, Master Ronald."

"Paco, listen. Tell my mother what happened to Mr. Jap's dog. Tell her I'm going to get to the bottom of it and I may be gone all day. But tell her not to worry. Now get on home."

He gulped and nodded. "Aye, aye, sir." And off he scampered. Whatever else could be said about Paco, he *was* obedient.

Jap's house was far off at the very edge of Puerto Del Sol, separated from its nearest neighbors by a twenty-acre garden farm with a windmill and a water-storage pool. It was a lonely spot Jap lived in. The road ended at his door and was never traveled by anyone else but Jap. I was breathless when I reached it and half sick with thinking about the sufferings of Lobo. Poor Jap—his boat gone and now his beloved dog burned, the only possessions he had! How he must curse the day he stumbled on the glass jar

with Neddie's map inside, the jar which made him pos-
sessor of gold he didn't want and the target of someone
who did want it, someone who had hounded him ever
since. Jap had been struck at four times: first by the night
prowler with the leather hand, next by the poisoned wine,
then last night by the loss of the boat which was his only
means of livelihood. And now the most senseless blow of
all—the malicious burning of his dog.

I dreaded to tell him the news. But he had a stalwart
heart, Jap had. I knew it and I was proved right; for if he
hadn't had a heart of steel and a will to match it he would
never have lived through that day—that last fateful day of
our adventure, a day I was never to forget and which was
so fittingly heralded by the nightmarish scene at dawn
on the quay.

I knocked loudly and called. There was no answer, so
I entered. My heart was drumming in my ears as I ran
across the bare little front room and into the bedroom
behind it.

Jap lay in his bed, his eyes closed. His pillow was a sod-
den mass of blood.

I couldn't look at him. I thought he was dead—so still
and white he was. For a few seconds I seemed to lose my
senses. The room reeled. Then I threw myself upon him.
I was sobbing like a child.

Jap's body was warm. I pressed my ear to his heart. It
was beating. "Oh Jap! Jap, you're alive!" I began to bab-
ble, talking to him, telling him to wake up. "I'm here,
Jap. I'm here." He neither moved nor uttered a sound.
Gently I began to cover him up, thinking to keep him

warm—not thinking at all, really, simply acting from some protective instinct.

Only then did I have the presence of mind to see that he had been struck on the temple—a heavy blow. The whole side of his face was bruised and the skin of his forehead split open. The blow had been struck a short while ago, for the blood was vivid red as it oozed over the pillow.

I ran into the patio to the well, where I let down a bucket and filled it. Tearing a strip from my shirt, I went back to wash Jap's wound.

As I entered the bedroom, all at once I saw the empty wheel chair of Valdez. It must have been standing there all the time.

The bucket fell from my fingers. I was hypnotized by that empty chair. It struck me as an object of unspeakable horror—like a severed limb, a headless man. The sight of it proved everything against Valdez. At the thought of him I was seized by a blinding hate, and at the same time by fear that made me suck in my breath. He wasn't a cripple. He was an active man and a giant, with a mind as cunning as a fox's. And he was my enemy. This knowledge was enough to wither the stoutest spirit; I felt as if a mad dog that I had thought chained were actually loose and charging for me.

I ran over to the chair and began searching its pockets and compartments. I had to find proof against him. Frantically I dug deep, scattering a dozen items around me on the floor, scrutinizing everything—books, newspaper clippings, a chessboard. Then I found what I wanted. There it was, tucked in a brief case—the map of the *Mary F.*, both halves neatly glued together. This proved that Valdez had broken into the shop.

I heard a noise and whirled.

There was Valdez watching me, standing near the patio door. He was smiling. His left arm sheathed in leather and the leather hand dangled at his side.

"You're rather careless with other people's possessions," he said lightly, indicating the objects strewn on the floor.

I said nothing. My eyes were darting this way and that, seeking a way of escape or a way of overpowering him.

He stepped closer. It seemed to me that he walked with difficulty. I thought of diving at his legs and upsetting him.

"Ronald, my boy," he said. "If you have any heroic notions of tackling me, I ought to tell you that I have a gun here." He raised his right hand and showed me a small revolver, carelessly pointing it at my head. "I won't kill you. I like you too well, but I could put you in the hospital for a nasty spell. I should tell you that I can hit a penny at two hundred yards."

I stepped back. "What do you want?"

"The map. Throw it over here. It's no good, but it's evidence."

I threw the map over; it landed close to his feet. He didn't stoop to pick it up. Instead he remained looking at me quizzically. "I see loathing on your face," he said rather sadly, even gently. "I'm sorry to effect you that way."

"How could you?" I cried, pointing at Jap. "How could you?"

He glanced at the bed. "He'll be all right. I gave him a tap with . . . Matilda." He joggled the lead-weighted leather hand. "He'll be out of commission for a day or so. But he'll live to catch many a fish yet. He's tough as a nutmeg."

"But why? Why?" I cried. Valdez was having that magnetic effect on me. He seemed almost friendly, reasonable. I had the insane feeling that everything could be cleared up, everything explained if he would just keep on talking in that deep, resonant, and intelligent voice of his.

"A mistake, I regret to say. One of the few I've ever made." He shoved the gun into his right-hand trouser pocket and patted it. "Don't try to run out on me, just because this is put away," he said. "A man with only one hand can't afford to be slow on the draw."

"What do you mean, a mistake? I don't understand," I said.

He took a few steps backward, still facing me. Then he picked up something from a bench in the patio and tossed it over to me. It was an empty bag, the bag in which Jap and I had carried our equipment the night before when we walked home through Frenchmen's Woods. It was still damp.

"A fitting joke on me for my misjudgment," he said. "Romantically, I had thought it filled with something more desirable than fishing gear . . . with British guineas." He laughed deep in his throat, a bitter chuckle.

"Never mind. The little man will be none the worse for his encounter with Matilda. . . . And as for the dog . . . what a pity."

I shrank back. "Did you set fire to the dog?"

He grimaced. "I? Of course not. I hate suffering . . . ugh, what a foul thing!"

"Then who did?"

"Ronald, my boy, when a man is searching for a sack of gold in a neighbor's house, shall we say, he doesn't want to be troubled by a barking dog . . . which might wake up the wrong people. I have a helper—a stupid dolt. I ordered the despicable idiot to get the dog out of the way. But I hardly expected such a spectacular drama over a dumb beast."

"Who is your helper?"

"You're very inquisitive, son. But it doesn't matter. I shall be leaving this delightful spot this evening—forever. My man is . . . Paco. Don't you remember that I found him for your mother?"

"To spy on us? But why?"

"To spy, hardly. He's far too stupid. But you may remember that it was I who suggested to your mother that she request the natives of this place to bring in old coins. I merely wanted Paco to inform me whenever anyone brought something in. You are mistaken if you think I intended to harm either you or your mother. I am a man who detests strife and violence. As it happened, I found other uses for Paco as events progressed. He is easily persuaded, as you probably know. I can't say, however, that

he performed a single task without bungling it. I threw
him out of here when he told me what he'd done to the
dog."

"Was it Paco who cut loose our boat?"

Valdez wasn't listening. He seemed to totter. A
shadow of pain crossed his face, making him wince. He
walked haltingly to the wheel chair and sat down, with-
drawing the revolver from his pocket and placing it on
the arm of the chair, the barrel pointed towards me. Ig-
noring my question, he seemed to read my thoughts.
"You've noticed that my legs aren't used to carrying me
yet. They've been useless now for two years, quite useless.
But I never gave up trying them out. I never ceased exer-
cising and massaging them. You must try massaging your
legs with only one hand. A ridiculous task for a grown
man. But, my boy, I *had* to walk again. I had to. Let my
case be a lesson to you, Ronald. The human will can do
anything—can make a lame man walk if he is determined
to do it. You see, there's a certain visit I must make in
Colombia, my home. It's a visit I must make standing
erect like a man." He laughed bitterly. "I took my first
step six months ago."

"But you never told anyone!"

"Who is interested in the pains of an old cripple? Besides, by letting people think I was still paralyzed I escaped a lot of troublesome suspicion—after I began to
pursue my goal in dead earnest."

Valdez's lined face had grown thoughtful. His eyes
seemed to burn like coals in the dim light of the shuttered

bedroom. He was thinking about his home, silent with his memories. The pleasant cast of his features faded. Some cruel, hidden emotion stirred him. He looked almost kingly, his great head lifted, his face stern and proud as if carved in granite. I felt an unwilling respect for him, an awe. I felt myself in the presence of a giant. Strength, dignity, suffering—they seemed to emanate from him, filling that little, barren room with a kind of splendor. I forgot he was my enemy, forgot that he had robbed, poisoned, lied. Had he asked me that moment, I would have followed him to the ends of the earth.

In another second the look of grandeur faded from his face. He returned to the present. I looked over my shoulder at Jap—half hoping that by some miracle he had regained consciousness and would come to my aid. But he seemed lifeless.

Valdez shifted in his chair and reached into one of the compartments for a length of rope. He was smiling at me almost apologetically. "I'm sorry. I'll have to tie you up for a while. It's either that . . . or a tap from Matilda. I've got to work unhampered for the day. I have a professional diver from N——. He'll be arriving in a few hours. And you, my boy, have to be kept out of the way. You're inclined to be somewhat of a nuisance."

Working with his right hand and using his false hand as a brace and lever, he quickly looped a few slip knots into the rope. Presently he looked up again. "Well . . . where shall it be? I think you might pass the time more pleasantly in the woodshed. I noticed an iron hitching ring in there, good solid iron, none of the shoddy manufacture one finds nowadays. I'll tie you there, if you'll be so kind.

He ordered me to walk ahead of him into the patio, telling me to keep two paces ahead, no more. He followed at my heels in the chair, the gun aimed at my back.

The patio was a high-walled enclosure about twelve feet square. One wall was formed by a series of three tiny rooms—the kitchen, the toilet, and the shed, which was the largest of the three.

"Open the door of the shed," Valdez ordered. "Keep facing me."

I did as I was told, though all the time I was trying to think of some way to overpower him. His legs were his weak point. If I could only unbalance him before he could shoot me! Unluckily the woodshed offered no opportunity. It was small, bare as an empty box. For an instant I thought of ducking sideways, taking cover behind the two feet of stone wall that adjoined the door and made the façade of the room. But what then? I could pull the door shut and lock myself in. His bullets wouldn't penetrate the stone, though they would easily go through the rickety door and could unhinge it. Anyway, Valdez needed no bullets. With his lead-weighted hand he could knock the flimsy lock of the door to bits with a single blow, as he had knocked our shop lock and Jap's head.

All this raced through my mind as I pulled open the door of the shed and stepped in. There wasn't a stick of firewood inside, nothing I could fling at him.

"Sit down on the floor," he said.

I sat down.

Valdez rolled closer until the bulk of his chair blocked the doorway. "This is an unpleasant task for me, my boy," he said. "It's a demeaning thing for a man to play at tying up youngsters. But . . ." He shrugged, smiling. "There's no other way, I'm afraid. In payment for this inconvenience, I'll satisfy your curiosity if you like. You may ask me any questions that are bothering you."

My mind was not occupied with questions at that moment, except the one big question: how was I going to avoid being bound and imprisoned? But by gaining time I might gain unexpected advantage. I asked, repeating my earlier question, "It was Paco, then, who cut our boat adrift?"

"Yes. I sent him to Frenchmen's Woods in a boat at sunset. You see, the map proved worthless—as you've already found out. Yet I knew you had stumbled on something. My boy, you must never follow a profession of deceit. You would be a total failure at it. Your thoughts are too easily read on your face. Adventure and excitement were alive all over that young face of yours, alight in your eyes. I sent Paco to await you. He was hidden in a cove near the spot marked on the map. He saw you disappear into the cave. The light showed up your every movement under the water. But then the fool lost what little nerve he had. He seemed to think you would come up and surprise him and give chase. So he cut the anchor rope. I'm sorry you had that gloomy walk home."

Valdez paused and grew thoughtful again. He made a sudden grimace of anger. "Ugh . . . that I am reduced to depending upon a craven fool!" He struck savagely at his thighs with the leather hand. "All because I'm half a man, a pitiable cripple missing one hand and with these quivering, feeble legs!" His face was ugly with despair.

"And the poison?"

"I'll say nothing on that, Ronald. Forgive me, but . . . such a confession might damage my chances to leave this town tonight—in case you should wriggle loose. I'll tell you that I've dabbled in potent juices recently . . . I . . . occasionally get depressed and had prepared a dose for myself, just in case." He stood up and I could see he was exerting great effort; his legs were steady, his step sure as he approached me.

"First your legs," he said gently. "Then we'll be equal opponents." He knelt down quickly; he was steady though the pain made sweat stand out on his forehead. Before I expected it, my legs were tied fast at the ankles. The rest was a matter of seconds. He bound my hands behind me, then tied my feet and hands together, also behind, so that I was lying on my side with knees bent back. After that he made me fast with a three foot length of rope to the iron hitching ring that was cemented in the stone wall, leaving me enough play to shift from side to side, no more.

"I'm afraid I'll have to gag you, too," he said, winding his scarf over the lower half of my face. "There now," he said returning to his chair. "I hope nothing pains you much. And don't worry. Your mother will send searchers for you before evening, and maybe before that your friend Jap will have come around. One way or another you'll be released. By then I shall be fifty miles at sea. I've hired a smuggler's boat. My diver will arrive by car within a few hours. It shouldn't take him much time to get the gold, now that I know where the cave is. Very clever of you to have found it." He smiled at me, his face sad. "Indeed, you're a clever boy, Ronald, and I'm sorry you couldn't have been my partner in this affair . . . very sorry, for I'm fond of you. I like your spirit."

I could do nothing but glare at him. I felt shamefully helpless. Worse, I felt ridiculous—bound and gagged, lying on the floor like a sack of wheat, restricted to expressing myself by writhing back and forth on the stones. Strangely enough, this very feeling of raging helplessness gave me an understanding of Valdez. He must feel this way all the time, I thought, his spirit forever imprisoned in a helpless body. Even as I lay there I admired him; I liked him, even as he prepared to rob me of the only means I had of saving my mother's health: for surely his diver would find the sack of guineas which Jap and I had tied to the anchor outside the cave.

Leaving the woodshed door open, he returned in his chair to Jap's bedroom. I heard him collecting together the items I had thrown about the floor when I was searching for the map. He locked the front door and came back to the patio.

"I'll have to bolt you in the shed," he said. "There's an opening in the upper wall; you'll have enough air. I'm sorry. But it's a precaution I must take, for you'll work that scarf off in about an hour and start raising your voice. The bolted door will muffle your shouts somewhat."

His hand was on the door. "This is good-bye, Ronald," he said. "It's too bad. You may be surprised when I tell you that I had hoped to make you my stepson." He stopped and his mask-like face, a face like an idol's, bent downward. "Yes, a hideous cripple like me can respond to a gentle spirit like your mother. But it can never be. My destiny has filled me with so much hate that there is no room for love to enter."

There were tears in his eyes. His face was gray. "Ronald, you must have asked yourself why. Why am I doing this for a few miserable pieces of gold? You certainly know that possessions mean nothing to me." He bent close. "Gold can not buy what I must have. But gold can give me the means to fulfill my destiny. Ronald, never allow yourself to become obsessed with hate. It is a killing master.

"I won't tell you all my long story. Only this: I was a happy man, a whole man in body and spirit three years ago. I was rich; my wealth was in the land, in a part of the jungle that I had tamed to be mine. I loved and was beloved. Then came an uprising. A man . . ." Here his jaws tightened. "A man envied me. He worked up my Indians against me by promising them things he could never fulfill and by giving them whiskey and inflaming them with hate.

"They killed my two sons, my little boys—suddenly, without warning, to wound me mortally in my most vulnerable spot, my heart. And when I sought this man out to kill him man to man, he had me shot from behind as I was facing him. He made me into the thing you see today. For many months they thought I wouldn't live. My wife died of a broken heart. Women do, you know, and men, too, in spite of what the doctors say. But I did not die. I could not die unavenged. While I was in the hospital this man legally took possession of my properties by means of forgery and bribery. I swore on the heart of my dead wife and on the hearts of my two children that I would never rest until I had avenged them. I borrowed to come here because of the map I had, borrowed to the hilt. Indeed, I have ruined a poor friend by accepting too much from him. Now I am going back to kill my enemy. It must be done."

Valdez slowly closed the door of the shed. "Goodbye," he said. The door clicked shut and I heard the bolt shoot into place.

10

I Make My Escape

Like the young fool I was I wore my trying to get loose. I strained my back and infla flesh of my wrists in the wildest efforts to break n The shoulder where Lobo had bitten me began After half an hour I was hot and panting and n nearer freedom than when I began. I had m ceeded in making myself acutely uncomfort and coal dust had worked into my eyes; my though dry by now, was twisted and half cho and my bonds were all the tighter.

At last I lay still on the floor, exhausted a my teeth. I found myself staring at the ti

153

opening high up in the wall, through which I could see a patch of vivid blue sky. I thought I had never seen anything more desirable and more unattainable.

I tried to guess the time from the angle of the sun's rays aslant across the window sill. It was still early. I listened, hoping to hear the sounds of some shepherd nearby with his herd, or a passing horse and rider. I could hear nothing but the songs of birds and the heavy creak of the windmill that stood between Jap's house and the rest of town.

I lay there for about fifteen minutes getting back my breath. Then, more sensibly, I set to work loosening the scarf that Valdez had twisted over my mouth. I moved my head sidewise and up in a swivel motion, but without success. Then I had an idea. I slid closer to the wall until I was leaning next to the hitching ring. By scraping the side of my wrapped-up face against the rough wall I was able to make some progress. I could feel the material slipping a little. The roughness of the stones caught on the threads of the scarf and, little by little, pulled it lower. I felt a spurt of new hope when, after twenty minutes, the scarf slipped down around my neck and my mouth was free.

I yelled for Jap and then listened. There was no answering sound—nothing. Valdez had said Jap would be out of commission for twenty-four hours. Hardly three had passed since he had been struck.

Then I called for help, shouting again and again until my voice rasped. The twitter of the birds and the lumbering noise of the slowly-turning mill answered me. It

was hard to believe that a town of two thousand persons lay not half a mile to my right, and that not one of them could hear me. It seemed impossible, for the little shed was fairly aquiver with the echoes of my shouts. I had sturdy lungs and a deep voice. But, of course, my voice was thrown back upon me, muffled by the four boxy walls. And the road to Jap's house was untraveled, because it led nowhere else. Anyway, the creaking and straining sounds of the giant mill wheel directly adjacent to the woodshed would have drowned out anything short of a siren. I called and called until my eyes were starting from my head. I had the eerie sensation that all the world had simply disappeared, and that I had been left to burst my lungs in a void.

When Valdez had locked me in I was confident that in half an hour, an hour at the most, I would be free. But gradually I began to realize that I was more firmly bound than I had dared to guess. The knots seemed to bite tighter as I strained at them. Valdez had known what he was about; he never did anything slipshod. And the peculiar situation of Jap's cottage, beneath the mill and far from any regular road, rendered all my shouts useless.

Once I accepted the situation, once I understood that I might remain here for hours—perhaps even until Jap got on his feet—I found myself growing calmer. My helplessness forced me to a patience I never knew was in me. Sooner or later I would be found. I wasn't going to die here—of that I was sure. My mother knew I was going to be away a long time—that is, if Paco had relayed the message. I couldn't be sure now. As for Valdez, who was going to rob me of my gold, there was nothing I could do about him. There was nothing at all to do but wait.

I made myself as comfortable as possible and looked at the sky through the window. Occasionally a white sea gull skimmed past, high up and far away like a fleck of light. I began to think about Valdez, about his parting words. The man had affected me deeply; I was still under the spell of his story. I found myself half glad that he was going to get the gold he wanted so desperately and that he would have his bitter revenge.

And yet, as I lay there filled with pity thinking of him, I felt a deep-seated repugnance for him and his goal. The singleness of his obsession was frightening, like a madness. He was a man destroyed by his own hate, just as surely as his enemy was to be destroyed by it. He had dedicated himself to kill. I murmured to myself that Jap was right; the gold was to cost more lives.

Then I thought of my mother. Even her sweet gaiety had been unable to melt the stone of hate lodged in Valdez's heart. I seemed suddenly to hear her dry cough and to see before me the burning cheeks and glittering eyes that had told me she was ill again. If Valdez took the gold—the gold in the sack that Jap and I had anchored— then my mother might die here—here, alone, far from the land she loved.

Like a tiger I began straining again at my bonds. I cursed Valdez, damned him with all the words I knew. It was due to his insane obsession that my mother had lost her spirit.

Valdez needed the gold to kill. I needed it, too, now,

and just as desperately. But I needed it to buy health and life for the person who was dearest to me in the world. Mine was the more just cause. I decided then, lying in that barren hut, helpless as I was, that I would get my sack of gold from Valdez. I would take it from him if he found it. I needed it more than he. If I could only get free before it was too late, before he had gone!

The long day passed. I felt no hunger though I hadn't eaten since the night before—only a weariness. Occasionally I dozed off. Sometimes I shouted; other times I tried again to break the ropes that tied me. But my only answer was the creaking of the dismal water mill, and the bonds never gave an inch.

The sun was descending and dusky shadows filled the shed when I heard the first human sound. It was a cry, a man's cry of surprise and fright.

At the top of my lungs I shouted: "Help! Help!" And then in Spanish: "*Socorro!*"

There was no response. I lay rigid, listening. "In the shed! I'm here!" I called again.

I heard the opening of a door—close, somewhere within Jap's house.

"Here! Here I am. Let me out!" I called.

Someone was in the patio, coming closer on soft-soled feet. A hand slid back the bolt of the woodshed door, and the next second I was half blinded by the evening light. A man stood in the doorway, hovering there. I could not see who it was, but I saw well enough the steel blade which he held in his hand.

The man gave a cry of astonishment. "Master Ronald!" The voice was Paco's.

"Untie me," I said, though I wondered: Had Paco come at Valdez's bidding? Had he been sent to "get me out of the way" as he'd been ordered to do to Lobo? The knife blade gleamed in the dying sunlight.

"Cut me loose," I ordered.

He knelt down and in a second I was free. I thought: Shall I whip him now, here—give him the beating of his life.

"Who sent you?" I demanded.

"Mrs. Vallings sent me," he said. "She's been taken sick. Someone thought they saw you go out with Mr. Valdez in a boat. He went out into the bay with a young fellow in a diver's helmet. But your mother said: 'Look for my son at Mr. Jap's.' She thought you spent the day with Mr. Jap, comforting him, after she heard about the . . . the . . . dog . . ." Paco stuttered. He dropped the subject and went on: "I had to climb over the patio wall to get in. The house is locked. And something's happened to Mr. Jap. There's blood on his head."

The air of worried concern with which Paco delivered this lengthy explanation was disengaging. He was too dumb to dissemble—he'd given himself away at the mention of the dog. I guessed that he probably knew nothing about Valdez's diver—the young man in the diver's helmet whom the townsmen had mistaken for me—nor about Valdez's plan to get away on a smuggler's boat this evening.

I couldn't trust Paco, that was sure. Yet I was going

to need his services. An idea had been forming in my head during those long hours when I lay bound, an idea I had to put into instant action if I didn't want to be too late.

I decided then and there that the only way to make Paco do my bidding was to dominate him, to threaten him. I had proved my power over him in the alleyway the evening the shop was robbed. I could do it again.

"Mr. Jap has been attacked," I said, pausing significantly, "because his guard dog was brutally burned—with kerosene."

I was right. Paco couldn't dissemble. He blushed; an idiotic grin—fawning, hypocritical, terrified—spread involuntarily over his features. He hunched up as if trying to make himself small. He took a step backward; his hand sought the door.

"Dog? What dog?" he said.

"You poured kerosene over Lobo and set fire to him, Paco. I know it."

He shook his head in a scared, wobbly way, but he confessed to his guilt by the question he asked: "How did you know?"

"Valdez told me."

Paco's face blanched. He half turned; he was going to run for it, but I grabbed him by the shoulder and shook him as one would shake a rag. He still had the knife in his hand, but he never thought to use it. A coward can't be made into a brave man no matter what his advantage is.

My fingers bit into his shoulder. He went limp and

said, "I threw matches only to frighten him."

"Listen here, Paco," I said, hissing at him, "that dog's suffering made enough commotion in town to have you put away for months. I'll tell the people. They'll lynch you. And I know everything else you've done. Taking bribes from Valdez to spy on us. Cutting loose the boat when Jap and I were under water . . ."

He hung his head. His face was ashen. He mumbled: "Mr. Valdez said he was looking for coins, he's a coin collector."

I snorted. "Don't play the fool, Paco. Anyway, whether you knew what you were doing or not, you're in this up to your neck, man. You can be convicted of half a dozen crimes. Shall I list them? There's destruction of property, accepting bribes, accomplice to a poisoning. . . ."

Paco interrupted. "Mr. Valdez didn't pay me much, just a little," he said, as if this fact would make his guilt lighter.

"Do you want me to take you to the police now? You know how fond they are of you."

He began to blubber. "I'm sorry, I'm sorry for everything I did. But Mr. Valdez seemed so nice, a friend of your mother's, a cripple. He just asked me at first to tell him about coins. . . ."

"That won't do. Being sorry isn't enough. What ever made you set fire to that poor dog?"

Paco shrugged. "I didn't mean to. It happened all of a sudden. I had the dog tied up near the mill. Mr. Valdez had ordered me to get rid of him, so I tried my pocket knife, but it was too dull. And after I stabbed at him, the dog seemed not to like me. He began snarling and I got scared. He was making a terrible racket and I thought Mr. Valdez would be mad. So I threw a can of water on him, but he kept on barking. Then I threw lighted matches to frighten him. Honestly, Master Ronald, I didn't know there was kerosene in that can. Flames started up all around, and before I could do anything the rope burned through and Lobo got loose."

"That pretty story is enough to get you put in jail for a long time," I said.

"Yes, Master Ronald, but I didn't try to burn Lobo."

"Now listen here, Paco. I may not take you to the police—if you'll answer my questions for me and answer them straight."

Paco literally jumped toward me and began kissing my hand. I jerked it away. "None of that. Get hold of yourself."

I handed him a handkerchief. While he wiped his nose and eyes I went to the well and drank a bucketful of water. Until that moment I hadn't noticed that I was terribly thirsty. I kept my eyes on Paco in case he might make a move to get away over the patio wall.

"All right," I said, returning to his side. "First: at what time exactly did Mr. Valdez go out in the boat?"

"About an hour ago."

Good. Something had held him up; his diver arrived late, probably. He had very little start on me.

"Whose boat did he hire?" I asked.

"Miguel Mari's boat."

I knew this boat. It was big but was only a sailboat with

auxiliary oars; it possessed no motor. He couldn't have been at the cave for more than forty minutes.

"All right, Paco," I said. "For the time being I won't take you to the police. But you have two things to do. If you do them faithfully and quickly I shall perhaps keep your sins to myself. Now listen carefully: You are going to run immediately for Dr. Sanchez and bring him here. Tell him to bring his car. Tell him Mr. Jap needs him urgently. He must come at once. Is that clear? Also, you're to tell him, in my name, to find out how the dog is."

"Yes, sir."

"You know where Dr. Sanchez's house is?"

"He's not at home. He's with your mother."

The mention of my mother almost caused me to waver in my resolution to follow Valdez. But I thrust the thought away. I didn't even ask about her health. Paco wouldn't know, anyway. The fact that Dr. Sanchez was at the Kansas City already told me too much.

"Very well, then," I said. "Go home. Tell Dr. Sanchez I sent you. Mr. Jap must be taken to the clinic. Can you remember all that?"

"Yes."

"Now for the second thing. Tell my mother you found me and that I'm all right. Tell her I'll be home in two hours."

Paco nodded. "Two hours," he repeated.

I paused and pinned him with a cold stare. "Now, Paco, I'm going to tell you something which you must

not tell my mother. If—now, mind you, it's only a possibility—*if* I do not return within two hours . . ." I
stepped aside to peer at the clock in Jap's kitchen. "If I'm
not back by nine-thirty sharp, you are to go to Gordo of
the gin shop. He'll still be open. Tell him I've borrowed
his father's boat; it's the fastest craft in town. I know how
to manage the motor. Tell him I had to take it without
asking his leave because I'm on the trail of his poisoner.
So, if I fail to return, tell Gordo that he is to come in the
Xara—that's the motor launch of the coast police. He's to
come in the *Xara* with the police to look for me. I'll be at
the spot east of Frenchmen's Woods where you cut loose
Mr. Jap's rowboat. You remember where that is?"

Paco said he did.

"Now, repeat what I've told you."

Paco did and very creditably, considering his limited
brain capacity. I had thoroughly scared him and he was
determined not to blunder this time. The alternative was
jail.

"Get going now. Go over the wall the way you came."
And as Paco dug the toes of his shoes into the stones, preparing to heave himself upwards, I said: "In case you get
any funny notions—that is, in case I don't appear at nine-
thirty and you think you'll just let me be, that you won't
go to Gordo (after all, why save me when I'm the only
one who knows your sins?)—I'll warn you now that I've
written down all I know about your activities and left that
testament in a sealed envelope with a lawyer to be opened
in case I don't come to collect it in person tomorrow." I

was bluffing. I had written no such paper—how could I have done so, bound here all day?

But Paco believed me. "Aye, aye, sir," he said. Then he scrambled over the wall and was gone.

I stood for a moment listening to the sounds of his running feet until they faded away. There was always the chance that pure panic would make him head for the countryside. But I had to risk it. I had no one else to depend on.

I set to work at once. There was still enough light to see by. Jap's lamp, his goggles, his knife—I took them all from the box in the patio where they were kept. Jap's swimming trunks were hanging on the clothesline and I took them, too, disrobing in a moment and pulling them on. They were roomy for me, but I had no time to cross town to get my own.

Before leaving I tiptoed into the bedroom, half-dreading what I might find, dreading to gaze again on the face of my wounded friend. As I stepped over the doorsill my heart lay hushed and anxious within me.

Jap had not moved; there he lay on his back, his eyes closed. The blood had dried now and half his head was encrusted with it. It looked black in the dim light.

I felt his pulse. It seemed to me much stronger, surging regularly beneath my finger tips, answering my hopes and fears. His stout heart seemed to be speaking to me, telling me it hadn't given up yet and that it never would.

I touched his cheek and spoke his name softly. He opened his eyes for a moment, but they did not focus. He was better, though; he would be all right until the doctor

came. "Sorry, Jap." I bent down and laid my cheek next
to his ear. "Sorry I have to leave you at a time like this."
I pressed my cheek to his.

Then I unbolted the front door, leaving it open for the
doctor. As I started across the field toward town I noticed
that the time was exactly seven-forty by the church tower
clock. Within two hours, before the long hand had
moved two full turns, I would be . . . either rich or
dead.

The light of day had almost faded; stars were palely
winking into their places. I hung Jap's lantern about my
neck and made for the quay.

11

The Final Night

The twilight hours were not busy ones on the quay of Puerto Del Sol. A few fishermen hung around, leisurely rolling up their nets or collecting their lines and baskets, preparatory to going home. I looked for Gordo's father—an old troll of a fellow who doted on his boat as if it were a favorite child. He wasn't in sight—a stroke of luck on my side. He would have raised Cain had he seen me untying the warp and spinning on the motor of his boat with an air of ownership. I tried to look casual about it—to sidetrack questions. A couple of fishermen looked over, but my manner convinced them that I had received

166

permission from the old man. They returned to their
work.

In a few moments I had weighed anchor, turned the
boat around, and was chugging away from the dock. She
was a lightheaded, dainty little boat; the *Zapatilla*, they
called her, the "slipper." She was a pleasure launch, and
she did look a bit like a lady's pointed pump. She lifted
her bow high out of the water as I gave the motor full
force. I left a white wake churning behind me.

Though the sun had set, it was one of those pale summer nights powdery with stars. The surface of the bay reflected the starlight like a mirror. I could see for more
than a mile.

I searched for signs of Valdez. I saw nothing, but the
Zapatilla covered the bay so swiftly that I soon discerned
the sombre outlines of a big smuggler's boat to the south,
lying off Coney Island. It was a long, low steamship, at
least a hundred tons—big enough to take Valdez to South
America if he wanted to charter it. And he could charter
it easily after he got his hands on the gold. Captains of
smuggling boats were on the ready to pick up an odd
dollar any time; they would go anywhere if you paid them
handsomely—no questions asked.

But Valdez himself wasn't in sight. He should be
somewhere in the bay in Miguel Mari's boat, if Paco had
told me the truth. I couldn't see a sail anywhere. Perhaps
he was lying to with sails furled. Perhaps he was off
Frenchmen's Woods.

If he were, I would come upon him soon enough, for I

had the *Zapatilla's* slim nose pointed straight for the red cave. I wondered what I would find there and what I would do. I intended to have my gold. Of that I was certain. I didn't care about the rest, but I was going to have mine, the gold I had pried out myself with the wedge and hammer, the gold Jap and I had sunk at the foot of the reef. And if Valdez tried to stop me or if he had already taken what was mine—I meant to fight him.

I sped ahead. Though I hadn't eaten all day and had had little sleep the last two nights I felt exhilarated. The sea spray touched my face like a spring mist. A warm wind blew over the waters. I had never felt so alive or had such a sense of well-being. I hadn't a thought to spare for the danger ahead, not the slightest prickle of fear. I was a lad with no head for gloomy forebodings. Call it the bravery of innocence; that's what it was. I knew I was being foolhardy, but the blood coursed through my veins like a mountain stream. I could have shouted from sheer exuberance.

I was close to the red cave when without warning the motor stopped. The lightweight little *Zapatilla* was bobbling on the waves like a chip of wood. I gave the motor a flip with the rope, than another. Nothing happened, not a cough. She was out of gas.

I called myself all kinds of a fool. Why hadn't I checked the gas before starting? But there was no time to waste in regret.

The boat had a pair of auxiliary oars—little sticks of things, meant for maneuvering in and out of its berth. I grabbed them and began to pull for dear life. I was al-

most at my goal. And fortunately I could see no sign of
Valdez or his sailboat. Or was this unfortunate? Had he
already taken my gold and left? Soon I would know.

After five strenuous minutes I was a few yards off shore
near the jutting rocks that humped above the cave. It was
out of the question to try to locate the cork-handled knife
which Jap and I had tied to our sack as a marker. We had
purposely tied it to hang a foot beneath the surface. In
that dark and moving water a sea hawk couldn't have
spied it. But I wouldn't need the marker to find the sack.
I knew the bottom here as I knew the features of my own
face. Once I got down I would get my bearings.

I shipped the oars when I was above the right spot—
or rather the spot I guessed by dead reckoning. I threw
out the *Zapatilla's* anchor and slipped overboard.

Sound carries far over the surface of the water, for
water is a better conductor than air. I hovered there for
a full minute, softly treading water, listening for sounds,
any sounds—voices, the splash of oars, anything that
might tell me where Valdez was. I heard nothing.

I lighted the lamp then and plunged straight to the
bottom. I had misjudged the spot, but not by far. A
couple of strokes along the bottom and I found Jap's
anchor. To my inexpressible delight, the beam of the lantern outlined our sack—fat, full, and bulging—exactly
where we had left it.

The sack was too heavy for me to lift to the surface
unaided; but I had counted on that. During those hours
I'd been tied up in Jap's shed, I had devised my plan.

I came up for air; then I dived and picked up the *Zapa-*

tilla's anchor in my arms. Walking along the bottom I carried it toward the place where the gold lay. I had to do the job in three shifts, coming up for air in between. It wasn't *Zapatilla's* anchor that weighed me; after all, heavy objects become lighter under the water. It was the infernal tug of the *Zapatilla* herself. Above me on the surface she tugged and bounded at her end of the rope while at my end, ten yards under, I pulled her along. She was as reluctant as a balky filly. But I managed. I got the *Zapatilla's* anchor within ten feet of Jap's anchor; and the *Zapatilla* herself was bobbling directly above. I shortened her anchor rope so she wouldn't have room to play tricks on me.

Next I searched for the line from Jap's anchor; it was lying curled up along the bottom like an eel. Grabbing the loose end, I swam with it to the surface and tied it to a brass ring in the bow of the *Zapatilla*. Now she was tethered fore and aft, as firm as a barge.

I went down now and cut the sack of coins loose from its mooring. I heaved it to the rough center point between the two anchors so that is was directly beneath the *Zapatilla's* hull. Two more lungfuls of air, two more dives, and my work would be done.

I had brought a coil of rope. This I looped around the sack like a basket sling, passing the line under the bottom of the sack several times. Though the neck of the sack was firmly bound with twine I was taking no chances of spilling my guineas out now that I'd got this far. When I finished, the sack looked like a Christmas package ready for the post office—but with a twenty-yard length of rope attached to its top. I rose to the surface for the last time with this rope in my hands and climbed into the *Zapatilla*.

I sat down for a moment to get my breath and shut off the lantern for safety's sake. But if anyone had been beside me he wouldn't have missed the grin of satisfaction that spread over my face. Everything had gone so much better than I expected. I had got my gold without having to fight Valdez. And he . . . well, he had got his and I didn't begrudge it to him.

All I had to do now was pull up my sack. I knelt down in the boat. Though my leverage was lessened that way, the boat would rock less dangerously than if I were standing. I was amidships, my back braced against the port gunwale. The line that connected me to the sack of guineas stretched across the little boat and hung over the starboard side opposite me. My weight on the port would counterbalance the weight of the sack on the starboard as I heaved it up. I had thought of everything.

I slipped the rope lightly backward through my hands until it was taut. Then slowly, meticulously, careful not to jerk, I began pulling, exerting a steady strength. The *Zapatilla* wobbled but there was nothing she could do. She was fast at both ends and evenly ballasted in the middle. Short of sinking straight under like a bullet, she had to bear the strain.

The gold sack swung free, ten yards down. I could feel it swaying and twisting in the current. Hand over hand, easily, smoothly, I lifted it. The *Zapatilla* was trembling. She seemed to cower deeper into the water.

Then with a sickening skid she tipped slightly to starboard. The sack had come out of the water. I felt the increased drag on my arms, the sudden dead heaviness.

The sack was stuck. I couldn't pull it aboard. Its neck was caught under the starboard railing.

Quickly I made my end of the rope fast to the port side. Then with my hands free I stretched cautiously athwart the boat until I was lying amidships like a crosspiece, my feet sticking over the port gunwale and my hands over the starboard. In this way I still managed to keep the boat on an even keel.

Groping over the starboard side my fingers touched the sack. I pushed it away from the bulwark, but it swung back. I hadn't the strength in such a position to lift it aboard. I inched closer. My head and arms were now hanging over the starboard gunwale.

The shift of weight was too much. The *Zapatilla* tilted to a forty-degree angle. Water poured in. I sat up—which took some scrambling—and heaved the sack aboard. Then I leaned backward to right the boat. She had shipped ten inches of water in as many seconds. She was almost awash and filled like a soup tureen, ready to wobble down to the bottom. I began bailing.

Ten minutes later I had relieved her. I sank back trembling.

Then and only then did I see not twenty yards away the shadow of a boat. It was moving toward me. Two figures were in it, one man rowing, and seated in the stern, clearly visible in the starlight, was the giant silhouette of Valdez.

I could not evade them, not without a motor. I waited.

A voice spoke sharply: "Look out ahead. There's something in our path. Why, it's a small boat!" The voice was Valdez's.

The rower paused and turned, but momentum carried the boat onward. It glided so near that I could see the gleam of Valdez's eyes—cat's eyes Jap called them—and the shine of the diver's helmet where it hung around his neck.

Valdez recognized me instantly. "Ronald Vallings," he said across the few yards that separated us. The two words were joyless, cold. He made a slight movement with his right arm, and the starlight caught the blue gleam of a revolver barrel. "So you want to be a hero," he said with a touch of irony.

I did not answer. I sat like a dead pigeon, the revolver aimed at my chest.

Valdez's voice softened. "What schemes are you up to, lad? You'd better go home. It's late and your mother is ill."

I spoke up. "I was just going. Good-bye for a second time, Mr. Valdez." I turned to the bow and deftly cut Jap's anchor rope. The *Zapatilla* lifted her nose with a bound.

Valdez stood up. His wheel chair was not in the boat; he must have disposed of it earlier aboard the smuggling boat. He was shaky on his legs in the rocking sea. The starlight shone on his mass of silver hair, making it incandescent. His fine profile—hawk nose, great firm jaw, and deeply-lined forehead—stood out in sharp silhouette against the dark hills behind.

"You seem very anxious to get away, Ronald," he said. The revolver was again trained on me as he spoke to his rower: "Bring our boat alongside. This lad is too clever by half to be out here for fish."

Miguel Mari's boat was maneuvered broadside to the *Zapatilla*. It nearly swamped me; the *Zapatilla* was half its length. The diver held the two boats together by hooking an arm over the gunwale of the *Zapatilla*. He looked scared and nervy. He didn't know what to make of it. He had been hired to dive, not to engage in petty piracy.

Valdez, standing, peered at my feet. He saw the sack.

"Ah, so I thought, Ronald," said Valdez. "You didn't come out here for the lark of chasing me. And you failed to tell me, too, that those abominable guineas were cemented fast in the vault of the cave. I've just come from carrying my first load to the big boat out there—that is, the first load my man recovered. I thank you for the gunny sack, though it was sadly depleted, barely a quarter full. This . . . " indicating the sack at my feet, "must be the top three-quarters." Valdez's tone changed abruptly: "What's in the sack?"

"Guineas," I said. A lie wouldn't have helped me.

"Ah, *those* are the guineas I thought I would find in that bedraggled sack at your friend's Jap's—the day Paco tried to take care of the dog, poor beast, and the day I had to tap your friend with Matilda. . . ." He paused and slightly lifted his leather hand. His face altered for a second; a breath of gentleness passed over it. "Was it only this morning? How long ago that seems."

Then he spoke sharply to the diver: "Clamp our boat to his." It was a matter of seconds. Two metal clamps, fore and aft, were hooked over the *Zapatilla*'s dainty bulwark. The two boats were made one.

Valdez sat down; his face and manner relaxed, now that he knew I couldn't get away. He waved the revolver rather gayly. "I'm afraid I'll have to have the sack, lad. The captain of the smuggling boat insists that he cannot abide in these waters more than another half hour. The moon will rise then, and the man's afraid of the shore police. He's got a load on his conscience.

"My diver cannot possibly dig out enough of those cursed coins in so short a time, Ronald; enough, that is, for me to ruin my compatriot, the man I told you about. I had hoped to make him beg for death. But that would require time, and time costs, you know. I shall have to relinquish the pleasure. But I shall have enough money to get to Colombia and to take his miserable life, which no doubt he sets great store by." He smiled at me; there was a surface gentleness, a wistfulness in that smile. Above it burned the eyes of a fanatic. "I shall have enough, just enough, when you give me your sack." His eyes burned into me.

I made no move.

Valdez stood up. "All right, Ronald. You'll hand it over now."

"I won't give it to you."

"Climb over and get that sack," he ordered the diver.

The young man, puzzled, hesitant, looked from one to the other of us.

"Do as I say," said Valdez.

Reluctantly the diver swung his leg over the clamped gunwales.

"If you come into this boat I'll split your head open with this," I said, showing Jap's fish knife.

The man shrank back; he hadn't bargained for this. Valdez coldly pointed the gun at him. "Do as I say or I'll shoot you dead, I assure you."

The diver, his face absolutely naked with fear, again lifted his leg to cross over. But I had been too quick for him. The moment Valdez's revolver was off me I had unhooked the two clamps. Our boats bumped inches apart.

"Climb over there, you fool!" said Valdez.

The terrified diver tried to span the distance, but I had shoved the big boat away with an oar. He couldn't straddle the water between us. With leg stretched out, torso leaning wide, the man stared back at Valdez, his eyes literally popping out of his head. He thought Valdez would shoot him; he expected to feel the bullet in his heart.

Valdez gave a snort of withering contempt, a snort that was almost a laugh. He waved the revolver playfully at the diver's head. The man hid his head in his arms. Valdez let out a peal of bitter laughter. "Get back in the boat," he said. From then on he ignored the diver; the man's show of cowardice made him beneath acknowledgment.

During these spare seconds I had scrambled to the

stern of the *Zapatilla* to cut her own anchor loose. My knife was poised.

Valdez shouted: "Don't cut that rope!"

"I must, sir."

Then: "Boy, I don't want to shoot you."

"You'll have to if you want my gold."

I bent then and cut the stern anchor. Valdez could have shot me; the starlight was clear and he was a dead shot. But an innate decency stayed his hand, for my back was towards him.

The boats were swinging wide. Instantly the dark seemed to draw a veil between us.

"You're going to give me the sack, Ronald," said Valdez, "or I shall have to shoot you, God forgive me."

I did not answer. I was rowing away.

I heard a deep, choking sigh and then: "I ask you on the souls of my little boys . . . my wife. . . ."

"I can't, sir, I can't." Tears stung my eyes.

I saw the revolver raised. Then in a strained, anguished voice came the last cry: "My God, my God! Spare me this last humiliation—the murder of children!"

I saw a flash of fire and felt a sting in my right arm. At the same moment I heaved the sack overboard and went with it to the bottom, holding it in my arms. I heard the second shot just as the water closed over my head, and the jerky voice of Valdez shouting: "Duck, you fool! Get out of the way!"

A body hurtled down through the water almost on top of me. It was the diver. I had neither mask nor light, but I couldn't have saved him anyway. His body washed ashore days later with a bullet in the brain. The frightened fool had got in the way; he had stopped the bullet meant for me.

I surfaced behind the *Zapatilla*, holding her steady and keeping cover behind her. Peeping under the bow I saw Miguel Mari's boat drifting seaward. It was thirty yards away. Valdez was sitting motionless in the stern. With his single hand he could not row; he knew nothing about the sail. And I doubted whether he could swim the distance to shore. He seemed to be doing nothing, just looking into the darkness. An orange moon was rising.

"Mr. Valdez!" I called.

He raised his head and looked toward the *Zapatilla*. He could not see me. "Are you hurt, lad?" he called.

"No." I didn't realize that I'd been shot through the arm.

There was silence.

"Mr. Valdez!" I called again.

He did not answer.

"Mr. Valdez, I'll row you to the big boat if you'll give me your word not to harm me or take my sack."

There was a longer silence, then: "I'm at the end of the line, Ronald. Please do not approach me or I shall shoot you. I wish to be left alone."

"You'll drift out to sea."

"No I won't. I am still master of my fate, I assure you."

I waited for some time, not knowing what to do. I felt I couldn't leave him to drift to his death. When I peeped around next, Valdez was kneeling in his boat. His head was bowed. He remained thus for several minutes. The boats had drifted so far apart now that I could scarcely see the outline of his figure.

Then: "Can you hear me, Ronald?" The voice was faint.

"Yes," I shouted. "Oh, sir, let me come for you. The big boat is leaving!" It was true. With the rising of the moon the smuggler's boat had winked alight. Steam was rising from her funnel. The crooked captain was making off with Valdez's gold, was abandoning him. "Let me row you home," I called.

"No." Then faintly, half lost in the sounds of sea and wind: "Ronald . . . I wish to say . . . that I have loved you. I could not kill you, I missed you purposely. How strange . . . to feel love again in my heart. It has ruined all my plans . . . I am lost . . . but I am content."

He stood up tall and straight. "Please tell them I *walked*; please tell them." Then he stepped, yes stepped into the sea and sank without a stroke. I saw it all in the light of the orange moon.

With a scream I propelled myself forward. I never swam so fast. But it was all useless. I cannot describe those next moments—even today I cannot. My pen falters and tears wet my page. It is enough to say that I was helpless before the implacable will of Valdez; I couldn't even find him beneath that dark and indifferent sea. He was a giant in all things, even in death.

12

The End of All in Manacor

They found me hours later adrift in the Zapatilla, unconscious from exhaustion and exposure. Gordo had come in the police launch, and when he failed to find me at the red cave he had searched the bay. They found Miguel Mari's empty boat first, but Paco, the ever-present Paco, it was really he who saved me—insisted that I had taken the *Zapatilla*. She was so light that she had drifted farther out, beyond Coney Island. I was at the brink of the open sea when the police searchlights picked up the little boat.

For many days I was delirious. My mother, too, was prostrate with grief for my sake. She didn't know why

I was suddenly so ill, but instinct told her that I had passed through something more debilitating than mere exposure. The shock of Mr. Valdez's death added to her despair. No one knew, of course, why it had happened; but his body washed up at Frenchmen's Wood's five days after that night, bloated and blue, yet with eyes open. Mother heard the news from Paco and it put her in bed. Her illness progressed by leaps and bounds. I never left her bedside.

I don't know what we would have done, what would have happened to us had it not been for Jap. True to his instructions, Paco had brought the doctor to Jap, and such was his incredible sturdiness that within five days Jap was out fishing again. He didn't know what had happened. No one did, for I hadn't been able to utter a coherent word. But wise little Jap, seeing the mask, the lamp, and the cork-handled knife in the *Zapatilla*, guessed. He went back to the shore near the red cave and recovered the sack.

And so we were able to go home, and I was able to become a lawyer as I am today. Jap did it all—not only by getting the gold, but by instilling me again with his wonderful zest for living, for the daily things of life. He booked passage on a ship for my mother and myself and he put us aboard—I almost as weak as my mother.

I have never seen him since that day. But he hires a scribe to write to me whenever he has an extra-big catch of fish. The letters are short, just facts; the longest I ever received was about the death of Lobo from old age. He lived on for ten years after we left, to the ripe old age of fourteen-and-a-half. Jap goes undersea fishing only for pleasure now—at sixty-five he can't keep it up every day. But he earns enough at the Kansas City. Yes, he took it over, to the surprise of tourists, who find he's never been to Kansas at all. I write to Jap regularly every month.

Here my story ends. Jap wouldn't take any of the gold. "What for?" he said. "If Jap want . . ." He winked. "He know where plenty more." But he's never been back to the red cave nor has he told anyone.

My mother is alive and well today. She is beside me as I write these words—still the same saucy, sweet woman at sixty-eight that she was thirty years ago. She never remarried. I did not tell her of Valdez's feeling for her, but sometimes she says: "You know, it's funny. I've never really thought seriously about a man since poor Mr. Valdez was drowned. Somehow they all seem sort of bland after him."

Beside me, too, are my sons, for whom I have written this tale. The eldest is named Valdez Vallings. Now he will know why.

ABOUT THE AUTHOR

Anne Sinclair Mehdevi was born in Manila on the Philippine Islands and grew up in Kansas and Missouri. She was graduated from the University of Rochester, New York, where she was elected to Phi Beta Kappa. She has done much work in advertising and journalism and served as a research worker on Newsweek.

Mrs. Mehdevi is the author of three distinguished adult books, all published by Alfred A. Knopf. She began to write after she married a Persian diplomat and her first book was a series of short sketches called Persian Adventure.

Over the years, Mrs. Mehdevi has learned to cope with being uprooted and transplanted at a moment's notice. Her eldest child was born in a primitive Mexican town, and her two youngest first opened their eyes in post-war Vienna.

The Leather Hand *is Mrs. Mehdevi's first book for young people. It is set in the Mediterranean, on a mythical island, which the author has placed near the island of Majorca where the Mehdevis have been living.*

A NOTE ON THE TYPE

This book was set on the Linotype in ELECTRA, *designed by W. A. Dwiggins. The Electra face is a simple and readable type suitable for printing books by present-day processes. It is not based on any historical model, and hence does not echo any particular time or fashion. It is without eccentricities to catch the eye and interfere with the reading—in general, its aim is to perform the function of a good book printing-type: to be read, and not seen.*

The book was composed, printed, and bound by H. WOLFF, NEW YORK. *Designed by* TERE LOPRETE.

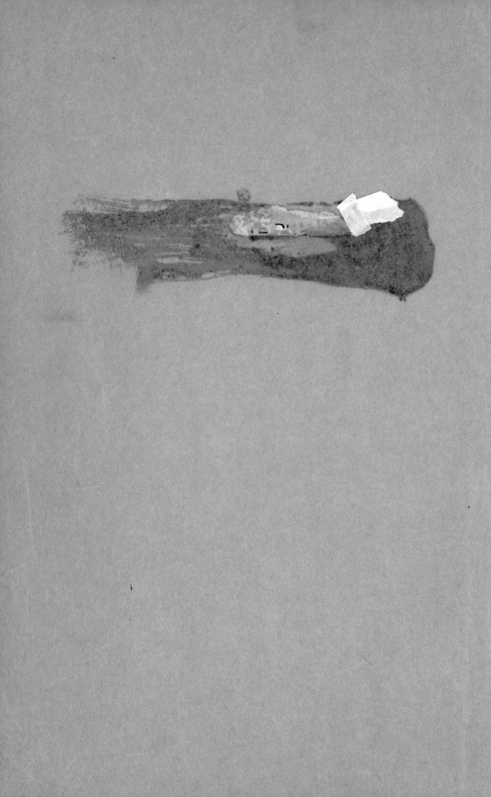